CHAPTER ONE

All three of us boys threw a darting sideways glance toward the house before skipping off the well-worn rocky path that led to the barn. There was an open area there that was just right for any kind of mischief our pre-teenage minds could imagine, conveniently out of our mother's line of sight.

I was dragging our hapless target by his neck while he stared into my eyes bewildered, not knowing what was going to happen. My eldest brother, Denzil, jostled along beside me, as did my younger brother, Samuel. They were ready to witness my making a complete idiot out of the little guy—who was actually a female—but that was really irrelevant. None of us felt an ounce of pity for doing it.

"Throw him down on his back in the dirt," Denzil ordered.

I did as he said, hungry with the glee that comes from having done this trick before and the anticipation of watching my brothers' faces. They were going to see soon enough that what I had told them was true.

"He's already confused," Samuel noted. "Won't be hard to hypnotize this one at all."

The chicken struggled at first, as if to show defiance, and then watched dutifully as I traced a circle on the dirt around its head. He relaxed, laid flat and stared blankly into nothingness like a robot in a comic book.

"Let's move away a little," Denzil said, clearly astonished. "See if he walks away."

I withdrew my hand from its neck, stepped back a few paces and marveled at the ignorance of this creature. His fluffy white form laid motionless, mindlessly under my control, as the three of us hovered around him.

Samuel was giggling like a little girl.

After we had observed this freakish phenomenon enough to satisfy us, I erased the dirt circle. The chicken rolled over and stood up, appearing to have no memory of the minutes prior.

"And that, boys," I boasted, "is how you hypnotize a chicken!"

"I'll be damned," Denzil said, slapping me on the back good-naturedly.

Samuel quickly corrected him. "Mommy says don't say 'you'll be damned' or it might come true." He could recite every rule our parents had ever made. It was a habit that my oldest brother and I were beginning to loathe.

"Shut up about mother's rules all the time," I commanded.

"Mommy says to say 'be quiet' instead of 'shut up,'" Samuel said. "'Shut up' is rude."

I reached out and gripped behind his neck with my thumb and forefinger as hard as I could to reinforce what I told him again. He cried out and wriggled free, running down the path again toward the house. Denzil joined me in the chase. Suddenly, Mother appeared out of nowhere and stopped our pursuit.

It was time to go inside for the evening. The smell of dinner hung heavy in the air just as it did at the same time every day. Our family's schedule for meals was just as dependable as the sun rising every day and it gave me a sense of comfort, knowing that. I can still remember pausing on that particular day to take a 360-degree visual survey of our home, taking in the scene of our magnificently weathered barn and the rusty metal grain silo and noticing that the corn was nearing its harvest time in the flat fields. I remember the struggle to feel the sense of duty to all of it and how eventually, I loved being a part of the daily activities that came with the farming life. Truth of it is--in retrospect, despite the physical hardships of our rather isolated and humble existence, we were living an amazing life.

I remember also being proud on that day because I had made quite an impression on my big brother, Denzil, by hypnotizing that chicken. Finally, I had demonstrated that I knew something that he didn't already know. As the leader of all eight of his siblings, Denzil was a wide-eyed white boy who, like me, was the son of a pair of

French immigrants who decided to stake their claim on an American dream on an 800-acre farm right in the center of the state of Kansas. We three oldest brothers were good-looking youths not only due to our fortunate French heritage that blessed us with tousled dark brown hair, thick eyebrows and ice-blue eyes, but in the way that young farm boys naturally become more sturdy and self-reliant than city boys. I had no doubt that someday we'd grow up to be handsome men with wives and families of our own. That was the main reason why I grew to understand the importance of the hard work necessary to keep the homestead running at its best— because someday we would each have a future even if I couldn't see it then; I knew there were better days ahead. The thing I never struggled to understand was my gratitude for having an older brother like Denzil. From the earliest memory, I looked to him for the strength and courage that I did not possess. It was just part of his conduct to be a leader to all of the siblings, and I was happy to follow him anywhere.

I wonder even as I'm writing this, with everything that our family's American dream encompassed, why I chose to center this story on Denzil. Why, even ten years after his death, do I still have a compulsion to talk about him all the time as if he were still living just around the corner from my house? There were six brothers and three sisters in our immediate family, all of them certainly worthy of me, their brother the writer, writing an interesting anecdote or two about them. To this day, I still have to resist the urge to pick up the telephone to call my oldest brother for advice. His presence lingers on me so strongly to this day that I have caught myself starting to do that very thing more than once, then sadly realizing that he is no longer here.

On the female side of our household, there was Lucy, who I always called my Big-Little-Sister (meaning that she was built fairly sturdy and younger than me); Marne, who was named after a river in France and the youngest, Odette, the quiet overly sensitive one. Except for Marne, who turned out to be a bit blonder than the rest, they all had the same dark hair and blue eyes as the boys. The remaining four boys were Auguste, who was two years younger than I; Samuel, who due to being affected by polio, walked with a weak delay in his step; and the youngest, the identical twins Charles and Cain. The twins not only looked alike, but they seemed to share one brain sometimes as they could finish each other's sentences perfectly.

After you get to know me and all of them, you'll probably figure out why I had to jump headlong into this unauthorized biography about Denzil—how, even as a young boy, he came to be the center of our lives. I'm not sure, if he were still living, if he would approve of my story, especially the part of it that he made me promise not to tell. If he were here though, surely I could argue my reasons for writing this until he would, I think, concede. It is, after all, partially my story too.

Only some of us closest to Denzil fully understood his depth of character and sense of duty, however bent it might have seemed at times. What's been written in the newspapers or what was told through the local grapevine, didn't tell things as they really happened back then. Some folks built him up like some kind of local hero and then, when situations became too difficult for them to understand or if they didn't want to look too closely at the truth—they tore him down. It was a cycle that our family grew to know all too well. I guess, when I really think about it, I needed to write his story to set the record straight; but I must admit there's another, more personal motive in letting all this out now.

I really just wanted to bring him back to life.

After the days of the Great Depression, even more immigrants poured into America than before, hoping to be an integral part of the rebuilding and success that would surely follow. Our parents were proud to be French, but also very proud to have become Americans in every way. The accumulation of land seemed to be the ultimate measure of themselves as new citizens to the country. Owning so many acres of land was an accomplishment in itself. Even some of the most successful farmers couldn't amass much more than two hundred acres, but my parents—I've been told mother especially—had insisted on accumulating additional land at a rate of a hundred acres a year, until the Second World War came. During those years, they found themselves more intent on survival than accumulating anything. All along the way, they were adding each one of their children to the homestead. The final total of eight hundred acres of land would become the lifeblood of our family for more than a century.

It was a tough yet idyllic kind of environment in which to grow up. Our whole world, aside from a monthly trip into town, consisted of everything we could see from the highest barn loft. From that vantage point, the distant horizon seemed like a definitive line that contained within it everything that mattered—the weathered barns, the maintenance sheds wrapped in tin sheets or other random roofing materials, the long wood plank and wire mesh pens for livestock, two grain silos, sprawling open fields and meandering streams, our two-story clapboard farmhouse and the carefully maintained equipment that helped us do our work. This view from the loft was the real perimeter of our world.

From these separate parts of the homestead we, as a family, could accomplished anything that we collectively set our minds to. We pumped most of the water that served the entire two-story farmhouse from a well one hundred feet below by plying a standing red iron handle set in a concrete slab. Another aquifer fed the water supply for everything else serving the farming operations. Every spring my brothers and sisters and I laid new or repaired existing irrigation pipes as the seeding process began again. Although we had a plumbing system in the house, we also had a smart wood-frame outhouse situated down a wispy trail past the barn. Over the years, my brothers and sisters helped our father with the birthing of dozens of calves, more than a few foals and plenty of kittens. Mother refused to be part of these tasks, stating that she had given birth to enough offspring of her own and didn't need to experience the labors of farm animals. I had a somewhat squeamish stomach back in those days and somehow managed to skip this part of farm life by throwing myself deeply into other tasks whenever a birth was imminent. In the evenings after dinner the entire family would gather on the front porch, the women usually mending clothing or reading books and such while the males discussed the affairs of the nation and future plans for the farm.

Often, at the end of the day, while the men (my father, my older brother Denzil and whatever hired help lived with us at the time) discussed matters affecting our life, they would keep their hands busy whittling wood chunks into objects for the children to enjoy. I marveled back then at their industriousness, how even when they were resting; they weren't really resting. There was an innate need to keep busy as if stopping for even a few hours might somehow jeopardize progress. Our father was quite proud to demonstrate that he could carve an entire linked-up train--engine, caboose and a couple cars in between--out of one long block of wood without ever cutting the pieces apart. I couldn't wait to be a grown man myself and be more important to the farming operation, even if I had the nagging feeling that there was a better life out in the real world somewhere. Knowing that I had to learn what my contributions would be by taking one step at a time, I approached my own simple wood carvings with a serious attitude, as if the care with which I whittled would make a statement to the others about my readiness in farming. Eventually, I became especially adept at carving whistles which came in handy to have in the pocket for me and my siblings when we'd get lost in the fields of towering corn.

The heavy wooden front door with its rusted iron hinges was always left unlocked during the daytime, as an open invitation to a long list of constant visitors. The general rule was to just barge in and whistle or call out a hearty "yoo-hoo?" until someone from the household appeared. Even though we and the family members who lived off the homestead each had a house phone, they followed the European custom of not calling in advance, unless they planned to stay for an extended period of time.

There were three aunts in the family--Lucy, Claudette and Odette--as well as an uncle who had also taken the long ocean journey to America with our parents. These four joyous souls were constantly around and were just as committed to the farm's success as my immediate family. They spoke often about the French concept of 'joie-de-vivre' and demonstrated its use whenever possible, by their gratitude, their passion for anything pursued and even in the eating of meals. When our great Uncle Charles came to visit, with his big booming laugh and boisterous stories, he helped us to forget the hard work waiting to be done and the serious worries that plagued our daily lives like the undercurrent of the black river, the one mother warned us to stay away from. I heard Mother say once that the worries on her mind and the black river both seemed to be invisible on the mirrored surface but she knew they had the strength to pull one underwater into utter darkness. When Uncle Charles was around, Mother's mood lightened considerably. He was a scruffy old man with gloriously bright blue eyes who, from my earliest memories, had seemed like a walking ghost to me. Despite his somewhat carefree demeanor, I also could tell that he was always there as a pillar of strength to my mother.

In addition to family members who came and went from the homestead, there were the adopted townsfolk who gathered at our house on the weekends. On most Sunday evenings, we'd have anywhere from fifteen to twenty people sitting around the wide front porch playing music, trying out the latest dances. There would be a bit of drinking, but it was kept in check as our parents frowned on drunkenness. This collection of people were quite similar to our family in that most of them had also migrated to Kansas in search of a life that would possibly be better than the land from which they came. They seemed intent on surviving the seasons of wild twisting winds, the predictably cyclical droughts and floods for the chance to capture the elusive American Dream. Most of these visitors were whole families, but some were just mothers with one or two children whose husbands couldn't stick it out when times got tough and had inconveniently disappeared, leaving them struggling to put food on the table. There was no hesitation between the rest of us, who understood struggling ourselves at times, to put out a full spread of our best food on the shared table for everyone. Mother used to say with a heartfelt determination that, at least on weekends, those children who had been abandoned would not go to bed hungry. In some way, knowing that we had corn and beef enough to share made me feel fortunate, even while

I understood that our family's bank account was often running low.

* * *

The three old aunts in the family used to tell a story about the last months when mother was carrying the yet-to-be-born Denzil, how her tummy would rumble and kick from the inside out, that he was an over-active child even before he first saw daylight. This gaggle of aunts was a secretive lot, as many women are when they group together in an effort to protect their families. These women had seen each other through their European childhoods, then married, then immigrated across the ocean followed by a series of trains to their new homes, then in the throes of labor, one widowed, one divorced and all of them dog-tired after working in the fields alongside the men whenever necessary. These weren't the lily-fingered type of women whom I met much later in life living in America's big cities. No; these women spoke about incidents and facts with absolute authority--from an entirely mystical place of knowing. These women could seemingly speak to each other without actually forming words. A nod of the chin upwards or a glance toward the floor when someone entered a room could be understood by each one of my old aunts without anyone else catching on. My brothers and sisters greatly admired them despite their tendency to show a lack of refinement and coquetry, for their lives had been lived immeasurably rich with limited financial resources and without much access to the world outside--yet they were so vibrant and cultured.

As these aunts often repeated around our imposing white wood-framed farmhouse, Denzil was a busy little cuss from the very beginning. In the current world people are apt to put labels on these kinds of children--things like 'hyper' or 'ADHD'--but in our time, families simply tried to find an endless array of activities to keep a boy like Denzil busy. If a boy like him didn't keep busy all the time that extra energy would inevitably get him into trouble.

He was six years older than me, so naturally, I followed his lead on pretty much everything. To say that I wanted to grow up and be like him was an understatement; however, I could sidestep that admiration too. If our mother ever caught us doing something wrong, I'd often try to use the distance between my brother's age and mine to untangle myself from punishment. "It was Denzil's idea," I would defend. "He told me to do it."

Mother saw through my ploys most of the time and would say, "Marc, you've got to take responsibility for your own actions. Denzil doesn't make you do anything. You control yourself." Then she would stare hard, but lovingly, into my eyes perhaps hoping that I would admit to my faults. Without fail, I would avert my eyes from hers to hide my fear that she might tell our father. While mother rendered a spanking with a very light hand, our father often grabbed the nearest thing to him for discipline. Sometimes we'd receive a couple lashings with a belt; sometimes it would be a rolled up newspaper. Denzil, for some reason, furiously hated the newspaper, declaring it a tool for training dogs, not children.

Our strict upbringing didn't stop at home. In our elementary school, as in all the American schools back then, there were a lot of behavioral rules and a real sense of control over students. In the Midwestern states it wasn't unusual to see a wooden paddle hanging on the wall near the doorway of a classroom, not just in our town but I had heard the adults talking that in other places like the Deep South this was common, too. Everyone's parents just seemed to accept that when children were in school, the job of discipline was wholly turned over to the teachers.

I often inspected these wooden paddles, these beating implements, for signs of terror—some had simple notches marked lightly as if the teachers kept a record of his or her successes with our training for life; others actually had the names of certain really bad students written in heavy pencil right on the front. I had a theory that the larger and darker the name was scrawled in lead, the more rebellious the child had been. It was no surprise to me to see Denzil's name on more than one paddle. Since he was the only Denzil in the entire county I knew for certain these bits of schoolroom history were attributable to him.

When the first three of us boys were still in grade school all at the same time, mother and father would often go into town for supplies, arranging for one or all of the aunts to stay with us after we returned from school. Without fail, Auguste, Denzil, Samuel and I would use these special occasions to push the predefined boundaries of our behavior. We figured it was probably the only time between school and the house that we could really cut loose. If we got into trouble when the old aunts were in charge, we knew that Denzil would be approached with an odd kind of reverence instead of disdain. They seemed to understand something about him that my siblings and I didn't because their leniency with the discipline certainly didn't extend to the rest of us. My sisters found our wantonly bad antics amusing and although they were too well-mannered to join in; they could often be found nearby watching everything we did.

Naturally, I looked up to Denzil and followed whatever he thought we should do at any given time. Tagging along with him when he drove the family's 1948 blue Ford truck into town on various errands became my treasured escape, a few hours at a stretch, always secretly hoping that some kind of adventure might find us. I was shorter then, and my brother always threw a sack of grain up on the leather seat for me to sit atop, so that I could be sure to see the scenery along the way.

Just bounding down the long dirt road before we hit actual pavement was truly adventurous enough for me. Depending upon how much rain we had at the time and the size of the potholes encountered, we could end up taking a ride similar to a roller coaster or we could end up digging the truck out of a grey sludgy pit. We always carried shovels in the back, just in case. Never mattered to me what might happen. I would sit on the edge of my seat, tall enough now to hang my arm out the window while beholding the neat rows of vegetables zipping along beside us while the truck windows rattled inside their metal tracks. This experience was always both a visual and auditory delight. Denzil drove that truck about ten miles per hour faster than it should have been pushed, singularly focused on getting to town. Once there, he often dropped me off at a nearby supply store to sharpen my buying skills. I worked off of father's handwritten list while my brother went to another location to meet up with assorted acquaintances to 'talk about business'.

CHAPTER TWO

It was soon after my twelfth birthday that our minor chores as children on the farm turned into my eldest brother and I gradually learning more about becoming real farm owners and were on our way to being young businessmen ourselves. Father had even opened up the financial ledgers showing us how each crop was tallied so that we would know if we were actually making money or not. One-by-one, he had also introduced us to his suppliers and contacts in town who were crucial to keeping our operation on track. Clearly, he wanted to gradually pull himself further out of the responsibilities of the homestead, so we endeavored to comply with every learning opportunity.

In our youthful naivety, we had helped enthusiastically with all kinds of labor on the farm, but now that we were getting older the expectations were evolving into taking on many of the same tasks as grown men. Denzil had always had an instinctive fascination with the various machines, tools, seeds and animals, but I had been the one who had always needed extra coaxing when it came to these things. As if he were trying to give the other siblings and I encouragement, Denzil began making elaborate hand-lettered, wooden signs and placing them around the eight hundred acres as reminders of what we should be doing or even how we should feel while we were farming. It was typical to see one of his infamous signs out in a plowed field in the middle of nowhere saying "REMEMBER TO GIVE THANKS TO GOD" or "FARMING ISN'T SUPPOSED TO BE EASY. IT'S SUPPOSED TO PRODUCE FOOD". Sometimes just the sight of these signs made me become more aggravated at the life I had been born into.

At the end of every workday, even with the added tasks on the business side of the farm, our hands were calloused and, in the dry hot summertime, the dirt in my nose and throat left me feeling like a tired pig. Our roles, even as we were supposed to be evolving into adult farmers, was filthy labor as far as I was concerned. In theory, I longed to be a part of everything, but the hard work involved always dragged my enthusiasm down. I would have rather learned about accounting, or stayed inside and cleaned house with mother than to milk stinking cows or harvest corn in the fields. I said how I felt aloud one day and my father sat me down in the kitchen with mother and three bushels of snap peas to shell. We shelled peas until our fingers nearly bled, or at least that's what I thought mine might do.

That next morning, I remember wanting nothing more than to sleep in. I was moody and feeling sorry for myself for having been born a farming slave. Father came into my room and woke me up at the first sounds of our proud prized rooster crowing outside. "The sun is up," he said, pulling back my blanket from over my head. "And, therefore; so are you. You're a farmer, too, and you have to pull your weight."

"I don't want to be a farmer," I returned, snatching the blanket back out of his hand. "It's not my fault we live in this godforsaken place. You and mother chose it. Not me." Before I could finish my sentence a strong hand slapped my mouth.

"Don't you ever act ungrateful about your place in life!" he barked. "You have a far better life than many. Someday you'll bring your own family to this property and you'll know that it was only through the hard work of everyone living here today that it kept going. You *will* get out of bed and you *will* do your part."

"Yes, Papa," I said in a small childlike way. After he left my room, I began to cry—not because of my father's angry hand—but because my childhood had simply vanished overnight, replaced by something between adolescence and manhood. In my heart, I still wanted to run around in the front yard in the evenings chasing fireflies and playing hide-and-seek with my younger brothers and sisters. I wanted to truly know joie-de-vivre.

That was the same day that I learned to turn over soil with a horse drawn plow. There were other farmers who already used a motorized tractor to do this, but Father felt it was important that I learned to plow a field in the same way his parents did in France. One of the neighbors had loaned us an amazingly strong Irish draught horse, weighing around maybe twelve hundred pounds and at least fifteen hands high. Together, he and I carved long straight rows into our soil that stretched on for miles, with me getting off the plow only when I had to kill a snake or to dislodge a rock that wasn't supposed to be there. At the end of that day, my back ached like an old man's, but I never once heard that gentle giant of a horse complaining, so I didn't either.

I remember walking the horse back that day when the plow broke, leading him by the reins toward the barn. He was a magnificent creature and I admired his devout acceptance of the farming life and his part in it. On the way, I passed by our storm cellar and outside, staked on a little wooden sign was another of my eldest brother's reminders for successful farming. It read, "IF YOU SEE A SNAKE, KILL IT. DON'T WAIT FOR SOMEONE TO DO IT FOR YOU."

The sign was typical of Denzil's approach to life in general—his steadfast view of how all of our lives should be managed for the good of the entire family. His role wasn't just that of an older brother; he was clearly the leader of all of us and even if I dismissed the endless advice and the constant push for better crops, I always realized that we collectively, as a family, had a well thought out plan that made sense. His endless energy often caused the rest of us to work harder than our natural abilities just to keep up. On days when we didn't have school, Father would drive all of us boys loaded up on the tractor's hay wagon onto a section of land, unloading shovels and hoes--and us--to dig up rocks for a day. Then he would turn the tractor towards the farmhouse. I would watch him until he and his tractor were nothing more than a distant dot before I began digging.

Even though I had resigned myself to accept hard work as our way of life, I continued to feel somewhat more like a slave than a soon-to-be-teenager, but I knew if I started to complain Denzil wouldn't let me say it. In father's absence, my brother always stepped up to the position of authority. He made it clear to me, Auguste and Samuel that there was no place in the field for the good-natured roughhousing that happened daily around the house. Those lighthearted moments would have to be set aside until just before sundown, when father returned with the tractor to take us home for dinner.

As summer came to a close, I tried to think of anything we could do in advance of starting the next school year that would cut down on the amount of waiting tasks so that I could focus on being a student. I wanted to do well in school for myself, but mostly I wanted to make my parents proud. Even though Aunt Odette and Uncle Charles had both graduated from college, mother and the others had only completed high school in France. I wanted to do more than graduate as Denzil had already done; I wanted to continue on to college to ensure that I would have better opportunities for my future. However; having to follow after my older brother's high school reputation as a rebel carried with it a certain responsibility to uphold any gains he might have made for the rest of us students, as well as a careful navigation to prove myself as a student who knew how to follow the rules.

I had never been spanked by a teacher, but one day I did manage to invoke the ire of my seventh grade teacher one day, by lying. Miss Purdy was 'purdy' to us male students or, in other words, very pretty. She had a body like the women gracing the pages of LIFE Magazine with the hourglass figure squeezed into a flowered daytime dress and shapely legs like a movie star. When I beheld her, it was the perfectly styled pouf of blonde hair that I marveled at the most. It was fluffed up into a tangled nest with a comb, then piled expertly higher on the top and pushed into place with a myriad of bobby pins and a coating of hairspray that glued it all into place. I had watched my Aunt Lucy create this very hairstyle on herself one day, but hers didn't even come close to the way my teacher had perfected it. Miss Purdy's hair matched her face which was fair-skinned and of perfect proportion with a flash of green eyes that could penetrate the eyes of any child and look straight into his or her soul. On this day I wished those eyes hadn't been searing into mine.

One of the students had brought in a fresh baked apple pie with a new, very odd concept--that it could be made smaller for an individual serving. This boy had somehow managed to bake this pie by using a scaled down handmade version of a metal pie pan that he brought to school for some sort of middle school show-n-tell. The idea of this was weird to me because we were certainly past the age of needing to perform show-n-tell with our school friends, but the boy was eager to tell all of us how this very small pie would somehow make him successful in the future. I had not eaten that morning as I had been rushed out the front door, without breakfast, forced by that inexorable master called time, to run down the road over a mile in the snow so that I wouldn't miss the school bus. My stomach had been rumbling all morning and when I happened to look in through the window of the empty classroom while everyone was out on library break—I spotted the miniature apple pie on the teacher's desk. I sneaked in and dug two fingers into it, scooping out the still warm apple filling and tested the flavor. It was exceptionally delicious. When I came to my senses, realizing that I needed to cover up my impulsive mistake, I began stretching, tucking and pinching the crust ever-so-delicately over the gaping hole until it looked new again. At that moment, the door opened and all the students filed in; wherein I filed in line too and found my desk at the same pace as the others.

What I learned quickly about teachers is that they have a sixth sense when it comes to any form of dishonesty. Just as our next session was beginning, the masterful seventh grade pie baker realized that his mini masterpiece had been gouged, he began to cry aloud like a girl and declare that it was ruined!

After a fast pass through all the puzzled faces in the classroom, the lovely Miss Purdy focused on me. I was growing into what the girls were calling 'a tall drink of water' and I slouched down in my chair trying to look as cool and manly as possible.

"Do you know anything about this?" she asked in a tone of voice deeper than the sweet one she used for instructing the class. She was beautiful but I sensed that she might be mean.

"I don't think so," I answered stupidly, instinctively sitting up taller. I swallowed hard, sensing the taste of the apples and cinnamon still heavy in my mouth.

"Oh, I think you do, Marc." She suddenly grabbed me by both arms and pulled me out sideways into the hallway, nearly dragging me from the speed of her walk. She pinned me up against the painted concrete wall.

"Are you lying to me?" she asked, turning my chin to face her and staring hard into my soul with those sharp green eyes. Over her shoulder, I could see the smiling faces of three of my classmates peering out the little square side window, waving at me.

"No. I don't know anything," I said, smirking at my classmates even though I was fearing what was to come. Everyone had heard rumors about one of the other students getting a hard smack across the face from her. I felt my body tense.

"Is something funny? You think it's okay to lie?" Continuing to grab tightly onto both of my arms as if the circulation of blood should be restricted, she began to shake me violently and I could feel my teeth chattering from the motion. "Don't. You. Ever. Lie. To. Me," she shrieked within inches of my face so that I could smell the alcohol on her breath that was much stronger than the sweet smell of her perfume. The combination of the two scents along with the rumbling in my stomach from having missed breakfast, and the extreme fear of being slapped all cumulated into a dizzy feeling in my head. I passed out.

When I came back to life, I was on the cot in the nurse's office. The nurse glanced around the room for a second as if to be sure nobody else was near the door, then she laughed. "You're quite the actor, young man," she said. "Good thinking."

I could tell by her expression that the nurse was on my side. Still, I didn't want to look like a coward who passed out in the face of conflict so I puffed up my chest and accepted the compliment. "I'm very smart when I'm being attacked," I said. "We have a snake on our farm who has done the same thing. You poke him with a stick and at first he puffs himself up to look bigger. Then, if that doesn't work; he just rolls over, belly up--pretends to be dead."

"Well, don't try it again," the nurse advised. "Especially not with that one. She has a reputation meaner than any of the man teachers. She'll probably be keeping an eye on you after this."

"I know," I said. I looked at the clock and it was time for the bell to ring marking the end of the school day.

"The school buses are lined up outside," the nurse said. "Go ahead on out there and get on yours. Be a better young man tomorrow."

"I will," I promised as I bolted for the door.

I meant to be good person always but I guess I had a bit of my big brother's rebellious side in me after all.

* * *

Even in his late teens, my brother Denzil stayed motivated to get to work whether it rained or snowed without regard to the weather. While the other guys who had graduated at the same time as he were either off to college, military training or just working part-time in town, my eldest brother spent every day planning how we could make our crops healthier and more bountiful. He had a real knack for finding the right mix of family members and hired help to get the tasks completed that would make it happen. If the land were dusty or if it were muddy from melting snow, it wasn't cause enough to make him change course. I watched him set out alone one morning in the late Fall with a couple of dowsing rods in-hand, a load of metal piping dragging behind him on a sledge. I caught up to him carrying a large mallet because I realized he was going to try to dig a well. Our well had run dry and attempting to dig deep into the nearly frozen soil, probing for water had very little chance of success. Still, I wanted to always try to do my part, even if I had no idea how we were going to dig a well without the massive machine made for doing it. Father had always been very good at dowsing for water, like they did in the old days, and although Denzil was fascinated with the process, he never had much luck with it.

Later, after hours of unsuccessful probing, our father was called in to relocate the project and within a matter of a few hours, together, he and Denzil managed to hit water and were running the pipes down together and attaching the new shallow well to the pump. While my solution would have been to give up and call the well digger, I admired both of them on that day, for their fervent dedication to approaching everything with a sense of order and a strong sense of purpose.

At least once a month, we would take the truck into town for whatever mission we might need to pursue. Denzil had begun to let our next youngest brother, Auguste go along now and then too, as a sort of nod to his approaching teenager years. It was not a pleasure trip to Denzil though. He made sure we stopped in to the cafes and diners where the local farmers congregated, keeping our family's presence at the forefront of everyone's view. Even when harvest time had passed, he still felt the need to give the residents of our county a pared-down report of our current farming agenda, then listen to what others were planning in order to get the most money for the next round of crops. He understood the importance of knowing as much about everything that went on in our county as the next man. In that way, he had become very much like our old aunts who inadvertently inserted themselves in all the local gossip and gratuitously dispensed wisdom to those in need.

While Denzil was there to absorb information and to foresee what might lie ahead for our family business, his two younger brothers were doing our part by testing the culinary offerings around town. For our brother Auguste and I, just having a slice of a strawberry-rhubarb pie that was reliably the same on every trip, or enjoying a cup of coffee in town somehow made these information sessions worthwhile. To sit at a laminated silver-trimmed tabletop with a bold red coffee mug in hand and sip the perfectly rewarmed brown concoction that we had created with the right amount of sugar, breathing in the steam floating off the top while the eldest men talked business, was a scene of pure joy. Chatting with the friendly young waitresses we met along the way, who seemed always happy to see us, was just an added bonus.

There was an illusion in those diners that the food and the drink served was somehow a better quality than what we had at home. Those formative days are beautiful memories that wrap themselves around my head, even now.

Of course, our real mission for hanging out in town was always to keep a thumb on the pulse of current events. In those days, the older farmers' faces were ragged and dirty and they generally stayed withdrawn from social connections with the exception of these in-town assemblages in the diners and the meeting halls. The idea of seeing myself someday in the future looking like them scared the hell out of me, but I didn't know any way around it. When we were sitting closely together as a group, we often overheard conversations about mean things that had happened to them or to someone they knew. Denzil especially loved hearing these kinds of stories and always mulled them over, discussing the circumstances on the long drive home, as if he were looking for solutions so that everything could be better for everyone. It seemed the whole country was getting wilder in their ambitions to make enough money to provide for their families. The older farmers' beat-up hands and crooked posture told only a portion of what they had to endure to survive in a land that shifted through seasons of blazing sunshine with no cloud cover to relentless wind-driven snowstorms. Many a perfectly healthy man had fainted while out in the fields because of the effects of a dusty Kansas summer heatwave and many had lost their way back home at wintertime when the snow blew sideways, blocking visibility in every direction.

By comparison, due to the fact that there were so many of us, I gradually realized that our family's situation was hard, yes; but that we actually had it better than most. We tackled the toughest jobs together and looked out for each other when hardships came our way. Those memorable trips helped me to return home to our flat and dusty spread of land, with a renewed feeling of gratitude for our family's farm. Denzil always said that optimism was the most important skill any farmer could own. I believe he was right.

The optimistic dream our mother had of coming to America as a young woman had turned out vastly different from the life she now lived. She also had gratitude for our farm but I was aware that she struggled to hold on to that dream sometimes. On those days when she was baking bread and the smell of warm yeast filled the house, she seemed to be essentially somewhere else. She would finish most days by cleaning the wide-slatted wooden floors with bleach water before hanging up her fancy embroidered cheesecloth apron and waiting for Aunt Lucy or Aunt Odette to visit. Our father would usually go up the stairs to their room long before any of my mother's sisters arrived, almost as if he sensed that the women needed time to themselves. After a few hours with either of her sisters, Mother would walk them out to their car to see them away, then return inside, silently heading up to her room.

Aunt Lucy was the one who could be reliably counted upon to show up with a supply of the latest copy of *Vogue* now and then to keep Mother's spirits up. Several times, I saw her put a few drops of what they called a 'soother' into a glass of iced water to help relax her on those days when she got sad. Mother always held Aunt Lucy in the highest regard, saying that she was a gifted bon vivant and a French gypsy who understood the true meaning of life and certainly dressing styles better than anyone she knew. Our father always said it was more like Aunt Lucy was a hussy. Anyway, I would stand off at a distance from the downstairs parlor and watch our mother thumb through the pages of these second-hand magazines, pen in hand, circling photos of the latest fashions in Paris and New York. It made no sense to me why she would even concern herself with that kind of thing, since such things would never be worn where we lived.

Eventually, as I matured solidly into my teen years and graduated from high school, I grew accustomed to the hard work and generally had stopped complaining. The value of a hard day's work and the honor that came along with it was now permanently engrained into my being. This was the life, as father had reminded us often that we were born into. In the evenings I would often find a place to lay down in the grass outside, just far enough from the house that I could still see my way back using the glow of the interior lights. Looking up at the stars, I would think about how vast the world must be outside of our farm, how unimaginably distant those stars must be. A lot of science had taken hold of my mind at school, especially astronomy, and on one night I had an epiphany that somewhere over in France, perhaps there was another young teenager laying in the grass outside his house. This boy, I supposed, was looking up at the very same stars that I now viewed.

Perhaps this youthful dreamer, I imagined, was wondering what life was like in America—perhaps even in Kansas. This sense of wonder, turned into an unshakable wanderlust. It began to take ahold of me and I made a vow that someday I would at least travel to my mother's homeland, to France, and set my eyes upon those same stars, but from another point of view. I don't know what I expected that other point of view to give me, but I knew that I would go there someday all the same.

During our usual dinner table conversations one night, I began to tell the rest of my family that I had a dream of traveling back to France in the future when I had my own wife and children. Father and Denzil reasoned that I shouldn't cause myself disappointment by wishing for any other opportunity. France was much further away than I thought, according to them, and much more expensive travel than any of us would ever be able to afford. I had, on occasion, heard both of them saying the same things to my mother, but it didn't stop her from also expressing how her heart longed to travel to Paris too, or even New York City, if only for the chance to wear fancy dresses again.

While I remained somewhat of a dreamer, my brother Denzil, became a stronger, more resolute and unstoppable force. As I watched him turn into an actual man right before my eyes, a certain amount of trouble became unavoidable for him. I should know—for most of it, I was right there with him. He seemed to have already found his standing in the world and was contented with it. He was also willing to fight for what he wanted.

Most of our encounters with people outside our own remote environment had always been the conversations and civil business dealings with the many acquaintances Denzil had made over the years in the shops or diners in town. As a young man now, he was fairly outgoing for his age and seemed to attract people to him, even the ones he had never met before, wherever he went. Unfortunately, a few people had nefarious ideas about the amount of money they would see him counting out on a table at the diner or a complete stranger would sometimes approach him with legitimate offers to transport illegal homemade liquor into the next county, using our father's truck. Denzil had his own way of speaking respectfully even to those who didn't deserve it and, by my way of thinking this high-mannered way about him emboldened troublemakers to think that they could muscle their way into our lives. I began to worry, so I kept an Old Timer pocket knife on me at all times. The hope was that I'd never need to use it, but I knew if anyone attempted to seriously harm my brother that I would—and within the space of a single heartbeat. Over the next several months, the air in town began to be filled with tales of trouble and rumors of trouble on its way. In the daylight, there had been a few robberies and many fist fights and even the good men were beginning to take to drinking in the evenings and doing things they regretted later.

We didn't think too deeply about what was stirring up a new wave of disreputable activities in town or to try with any real effort to completely avoid them. Some said that it was a nervousness creeping into folks because of conversations happening nationally about possible impending war. When I told my brother that I was becoming more and more leery of our trips because of this talk of escalating danger, he squared me away with his usual straightforward advice. "It's our duty to keep going about our chores that keep the farm business running and not be derailed by what other people may or may not be speculating or trying to do," Denzil had told me. "As far as looking after our interests, there's a few new guys that have come into our county who are only trying to cut in on other people's money instead of earning it for themselves. Much easier that way is what they're thinking. What I'm thinking is that if they try anything dangerous with us, it could be the last thing they do."

It wasn't too long before that day I feared came to pass. Early one morning we showed up at the train station to ship our potatoes out to a fellow located in New York. All at once, a truck pulled up with three large ruffians from another town who ordered us to give them our crop.

"I'll be taking that entire truckload of whatever you have there," the leader said to my brother and me. He was wielding a long fileting knife.

"You joking?" Denzil asked, climbing out of the truck with a metal club in-hand behind his back. "You're gonna' risk your life to hijack my family's crop of potatoes?" With his free hand he lifted the cover off the crates and pulled one of the potatoes out, to show them our cargo. "These are potatoes, man, they're not gold."

My brother, as smart as he usually was, simply couldn't fathom why someone would want to steal food.

Clearly, the way these intruders saw it, those brown potatoes were golden nuggets. The other two ruffians quickly produced knives from their pockets to help us understand that. "Good enough and worth money. I'm taking all of them," the leader repeated. The other two inched closer toward me as my heart sunk into my stomach.

Instead of fighting and with no warning to me, Denzil suddenly jumped back into the driver's seat and slammed the door. I bolted like a jackrabbit around to the passenger's side and did the same. The truck was thrown into gear even before I heard the engine start. With dirt flying in every direction, he drove headlong into the men who were trying to block our exit, grazing one of them with the truck enough that they all jumped away for the ground. He didn't stop to check for injuries.

We were halfway home before either of us spoke. "Imagine that," Denzil said finally. "Grown men foolish enough to risk their lives over crates of potatoes. Damn fools they were. We set hundreds of feet of irrigation pipe this season to keep that crop going. I'm damned if they're going to get it by flashing knives at us."

"We'll go back to sell them tomorrow?" I asked.

"Yeah. Could have sold them yet today, but for sure those guys would have been trying to track us. Tomorrow we'll haul these crates out again," he said. "And don't worry about these sorts of troubles. I'll sure be better prepared to take care of us tomorrow."

It should have been our father taking care of us in troubled times, but I had more faith in Denzil's handling of financial transactions anyway, even if he were just barely into adulthood himself. We did return the next day and sold our potatoes. My brother had a loaded shotgun stashed under the bench seat of the truck as insurance.

Mother must have had the same faith in Denzil that I had because she had never asked anyone but him to drive the produce into town for sale. With the added element of possible danger, I found myself becoming oddly even more interested in the business side of farming and hoped that someday I'd be the one representing our family's crops to buyers. Most of all, I couldn't wait to drive the truck.

Over the next couple of years, there began to be very real and intense talk in the world, in town and in the newspapers of a serious sort. It seemed that the leaders of the world were talking about the possibility of imminent war and my parents often debated the possible effects of a war over dinner, worried about how the eventual rationing of supplies, if it happened, would impact us. People had already begun to hoard supplies and stock up on food, especially.

On one afternoon, the Mazur brothers from Poland who were known to be a belligerent and bullying lot, wandered onto our property to go deer hunting. Denzil and I had been in some serious fist-fights with these brothers as we passed through high school on more than one occasion. Their family owned a sprawling ranch-styled property about a fourth the size of ours in the same county, but they never seemed to contain their activities to their own land.

The father to these two guys was known locally as 'Old Man Mazur'. He was a massive man with hands like boulders who had worked on oil rigs most of his life and was known for having a cruel streak when it came to disciplining his own children. Everyone knew it was he who had made those two brothers mean. He had even been known to strike a couple of the neighborhood kids who had visited their house on more than one occasion, if they misbehaved. Anyone who in his view, 'got out of line' was going to get straightened out. Lately, he had taken up politics and our father had said it was the perfect career for him.

It was a dreary fall day when Denzil and I heard a gunshot ring out from the corner of our cornfield. We navigated over in the general direction, running at a full pace, then proceeded ever-so-carefully to the place where the oldest Mazur brother knelt beside the deer he had killed.

He looked up when he saw Denzil and jumped up to his feet next to the carcass.

"That's our deer on our property," Denzil said straight away. "You can't take it with you."

"It's my deer. I shot it," he said bracing for a fight. He outweighed my older brother by more than a few pounds, but he already sensed that in a fair fight, Denzil could take him easily.

I felt anxious knowing that I might have to fight his younger brother who was now ambling up the hill and seeing all of us together. I motioned with my hand for him to stay out of it and gave him as threatening of a look as I could muster.

Denzil looked down at the deer.

"It's meat for our family," the older brother said, trying to force a reaction of sympathy from Denzil. "I'll just take it and be gone."

Denzil wasn't going to let it go. "No. Now, we need to settle this with a competition, if you're game."

"And what might that be?"

"Well, we'll play a little game to see who's tougher. You were always up for that in school when you wanted to bully someone, right?"

"Damn right; I was that for sure," he said, clearly proud of it. "I'll play your game, whatever it is, and take the deer for it. So what shall we do to prove who is tougher?" a grin crossed his lips and I could see that he relished the idea of beating Denzil at anything, for any reason.

Denzil looked over at the younger Mazur brother. "Well, we'll take turns letting the younger of our brothers kick us in the nuts. Whoever is left standing at the end gets the deer."

"Hah! A rotten game it is! But no problem for me." He glanced nervously at me and I readied myself with glee.

"Marc goes first," Denzil announced decidedly. Before anything else could be said, I walked over and kicked the meat-headed guy squarely in the nuts. He hit the ground immediately, writhing in pain but held back vocalizing exactly how much. After a few minutes, he gathered his strength again. He stood up, albeit visibly weaker than before and straightened his posture.

"Our turn now," he said defiantly, cutting his eyes over to his younger brother who was already stepping up towards Denzil for his turn.

Just before he got to Denzil, my brother put his hands up and said, "Okay I give up. You guys win! Take the damn deer. You got five minutes to get him off our property before I start shooting."

As the two Mazur brothers looked at each other in astonishment, I followed my brother, going quickly back into the corner of the cornfield as when we had arrived. After a few paces, we were shielded from their sight by the tall green pillars overhead. We began to run, laughing hysterically all the way back to the barn.

"You won't be telling mother or anyone else for that matter," Denzil said as I jostled along beside him.

"Agreed," I said.

* * *

It wasn't long before the number of people becoming more brazen in their methods to sneak onto our property or to try to dupe us out of our money or our crops multiplied. Additionally, we grew to expect that every time we went into town we would have to be on guard. There were even more desperate souls coming out of the shadows, who eventually tracked us out to our farm. It was as if they preferred to go straight to the source of our bounty now than to wait for our random appearances in town.

Once, a group of thieves sneaked out onto our property in the middle of the night. Denzil had heard in advance, through someone of his acquaintance, that a group of out-of-town men had a coordinated plan to steal our freshly harvested crops. While we would be sleeping one night, the plan was to shuttle several crates of our produce onto the backs of two flatbed trucks that would be parked a short distance down the road. Denzil found out exactly on which night they were coming and where they would be parked. Then, he spent a whole day building a wooden watchtower up in one of our highest trees.

Under the moonlight, just as we were warned, we watched two men transfer the first of our loaded produce crates up onto an open horse-drawn wagon. Then, they quietly inspected the remaining crates, readying themselves to haul them up onto the wagon too. Their plan to disappear back down the road and load up the waiting trucks seemed flawless. Denzil and I sat in the watchtower without moving to stop them. Before they even got the first batch of crates completely loaded, we heard their screams because they had stepped into the wicked iron jaws of the coiled-spring coyote traps we had set under the dirt that afternoon. Denzil waited a few minutes before climbing down from the tree, then responded with a shotgun in his hands. I followed, and when we caught up to them, he handed the gun to me. With my knees shaking and my guts wrenching, I trained it on them and prepared myself mentally that I might actually have to use it. Without saying a word, he walked over to the thieves, one at a time, and opened the traps up enough to free their legs. "Now look me in the eyes and listen carefully," my brother instructed them. "You go tell your thieving friends that if anyone steals from us, this isn't the worst that's going to happen—next time I'll shoot you." They were in obvious pain as they inched away from my brother and I, both appearing to have damaged ankles. Without uttering a single word, they managed to hobble back up to walk their horse and their open wagon down the road toward the trucks.

My brother and I watched the slight dust trail that was kicked up under the moonlight as they disappeared from view. Denzil turned back towards the farmhouse and I followed. He seemed to want to lessen our cruelty in utilizing the traps on the men. "If it was someone hungry, I might've given them a batch of food. But a thief is yet another thing. That's nothing we can tolerate."

We found our mother in the kitchen, sharing a baked dessert with Aunt Lucy. I relayed everything that had happened with as much detail and excitement as I could manage. Mother was clearly aghast and gave Denzil a weary look. However; I was proud to have been a part of it. "That's what they deserve for trying to steal from us," I said. "They'd better go on back and tell the rest of those who would try it what's going to happen, right Denzil?"

"Thieves don't measure all the possibilities of what can go wrong with their plan," he said. "They're so bent on the stealing part they believe they're invincible. If there's a next time for that bunch I'll be putting a bullet in their heads. I'll make 'em into scarecrows for the cornfields."

Then just as she always did when Denzil reacted to things like that or when anyone for that matter, showed anger, I noticed that Aunt Lucy poured a glass of ice water. Before giving it to Mother, she put a drop of the soother in it.

Trying to make light of the weird mood in the room, I laughed at the situation. "At least everyone will know who the thieves are now, due to their limpy legs."

My attempt at humor fell flat and the room remained silent. Denzil motioned for me to leave the women alone and follow him outside as we returned to the area of the new watchtower. He quietly went about springing the remaining iron traps with a stick, then rehanging them in the barn before corralling me back into the house for the evening. "It's the way of the corn," he said, as if to himself and me all at once. He had a way of being finished with a matter and looking into the next morning as if someday our lives would be something other than what we had been handed.

I didn't know what that meant, but I could tell that he wanted to believe that better days were just around the corner, whereas I had tucked away my secret dream of traveling to France. My acceptance that this life was as good as any other was only temporary.

Along with this marked increase in the hardships coming at us which was also around the time Denzil turned twenty-one; he had referred often to the troubles as 'happenings'. It was during this time of uncertainty that he began to acknowledge whatever came our way by saying that it was "just the way of the corn". This steadfast mantra of sorts, adopted in his early manhood, was a refusal to admit defeat at all costs. It was his mantra to calm everyone around us when things got out of control or if situations turned unexpectedly bad. "It's the way of the corn," Denzil would state with authority; then he'd take care of whatever had befallen us and be finished with it.

My three sisters and the other four brothers didn't understand his meaning any more than I did. He never offered to explain, even when we questioned what he meant. It wouldn't be until a few years later, after he had been forced to become a fighting man at the great steely hand of the U. S. Army draft and fought in two horrific battles in the European theater that he would explain to me exactly what corn had to do with anything that happened in our humbled lives. As far as the rest of us were concerned, corn was no different than potatoes. It was simply a commodity that put money into our homestead, providing for us and our livestock.

CHAPTER THREE

Denzil came home one afternoon and after making sure he had seated the whole family comfortably around the front living room, announced to our family that he had been accepted into the service of the United States Army. Mother, fearing this was the case, had already shown me the envelope when it came in the mail before she had given it to him. I wanted to correct him and say that he really hadn't applied, but rather he had been drafted, but I let my beloved brother face it in his own way.

I can't recall the number of times before Denzil left with the Army that he went out for a night in town that ultimately ended up in some kind of altercation. It was as if he had thought about not being able to return home one day, that he was hell-bent on packing all the action into his short time in Kansas while he could. He typically began the story afterwards with, "It wasn't my fault..." before launching into a million reasons why the other guys had it coming. I had become acutely aware that he and his friends had started to drink a bit and that this contributed to unclear thinking in whatever was said or done. However, right or wrong; I agreed with him as a matter of loyalty. Usually those who made the choice to tangle with my brother did have it coming and he, who was now a lean-muscled wedge of a man, was one who was going to give it to them.

Maybe it was the way he automatically moved himself to the front of the pack when a bunch of us young wolves were out on the prowl--whenever we'd get loose from the farm on a late Saturday afternoon. Maybe it was the wide inviting grin that would cross his lips when he foresaw someone itching for a fight and heading our way. Perhaps it was the way his strong blue eyes flickered and danced, as if there was an element of fun to it all. Whatever moved people to single out Denzil to work out their idiosyncrasies (as he called them) was a force greater than my own, because it didn't seem to matter what I tried to do to redirect their concerns elsewhere.

Our parents had officially allowed me to go into town for evenings out with my brother and his friends during this period of time, even if I was still under the legal age for bars. I was physically matured enough now that nobody ever questioned me for being there and I know my presence gave my mother at least, some comfort. Maybe too, they were giving us the opportunity to make some fond memories together before he went away for a long time. On some Saturday nights, my brother and I returned home beat up or dripping blood from our nose or with some dirt-filled laceration of the skin. Mother cleaned us up a couple of times and then, after realizing it was becoming our weekend sport, she declined to offer help. As a matter of fact, she often wouldn't even look at us if she could tell we had been drinking too much. I can still see her, pointing her finger toward the wooden staircase leading up to our shared bathroom and bedrooms. Looking back, it must have broken her heart seeing two adult boys-whom she had tried to infuse with the education, genteelness and gracious ways of her French culture--turning into regular backwoods heathens. The guilt from this often caused me to rise early on Sunday mornings, even when I didn't feel like it, to accompany my mother and her grown siblings to the

Lutheran church in town. Uncle Charles made the entire Sunday service worthwhile when he'd belt out the hymns like an opera singer. He had a wonderful tenor voice with a volume unmatched by any other man in attendance. I'd stand between Mother and her sisters, singing those beautiful gospel hymns with a purposely overblown reverence. I figured it might give her hope that at least a small part of me was redeemable.

It wasn't only the fun of drinking and fist-fighting that we were searching for on our weekend adventures away from the house. My brother and I had taken our fair share of rounds with the local girls in town, too. I tended to drift from one to the next, not being able to decide if I really had the depth of character it took to settle down in any kind of real relationship. I have to say that I was the better looking of the two of us, so it was like taking my pick of the lot sometimes.

Denzil had been capable of forming relationships with females, since high school; some had lasted as long as eight months or even a year. Even without being blessed with my natural good looks, he had made up for any shortcomings with that broad genuine smile and a mind like quick-silver that could hold any conversation a lady might want to have. I think his heart was searching for an elusive kind of female, who wasn't likely to exist in the rural farmlands we called our home. Now that we were older, we began to venture outside the borders of our town and into the next one trying to meet new young ladies. There was one particular special girl Denzil saw regularly for a long time, who lived in a town about an hour from us—in Kansas City. Her name was Bernadette.

She was one of those girls who had become a full-fledged woman long before all the others. Even her walk was special. She had a long, deliberate, leggy stride that reminded me of the water birds that used to land on the tops of the corn stalks and navigate the field, walking from one silky tip of corn to another. When she talked, her melodic voice encircled your head and you felt almost hypnotized. She had hypnotized my older brother and it was sheer joy for me to stand by with my various dates coming and going, watching it all unfold.

I knew he was truly in love with Bernadette because I could see happiness multiplying in his eyes. I knew he was in love with her when he would randomly talk about her as we were driving back home late at night. I could be talking about beans or bacon or bicycles and Denzil would steer the conversation somehow so that it related to Bernadette. Suddenly, my hard-working and focused brother had become more of a daydreamer than I had ever been. He would whisper her name while he helped me stack the tight-bound bales of hay in the barn or he would write it in the dirt with a stick. Once, I walked up on him lying out in the open fields, looking up at the clouds gliding past, and he was repeating her name over and over, slowly, and with added enunciation.

Since we couldn't always find the time or the means to travel to meet up with Bernadette, however; Denzil also spent his free time in our town with another young lady named Ophelia. Now, that is pronounced 'Oh-Feel-Ya' and we all enjoyed being snarky with the fact that there was a lot of feeling going on between my brother and this young lady. Me and some of the other local boys even made her name into a song: "Oh Feel Ya, Can I Feel Ya Tonight", etc, etc... The song always started like that and words were changed to fit that particular day. Eventually my brother Auguste and I began to add new lines to it every time we knew Denzil was heading out for an evening with her. We made certain that we stopped short of bordering real vulgarity though, because my oldest brother didn't tolerate vulgar-speak about women. We could disparage a man's personhood right down into the dirtiest mud hole around, but speaking too far in the trenches about a woman would get us straightened out real quick.

There were long days when Ophelia would get her mother to drive her all the way across town to drop her off for a visit at our property. I can still see her trudging down the dusty driveway wearing a short-sleeved button down shirt and a skirt that ended, not below her knees like all the proper girls wore back then, but about two inches above the knees. Always, she would be toting the little round leather baby blue purse that Denzil said matched her eyes. After exchanging pleasantries with my parents and acknowledging all the brothers and sisters, she would turn her attentions exclusively onto Denzil. The two of them would climb up on the tractor, sitting on the big metal seat side-by-side, and disappear into the rows of corn for hours at a time.

Then by the following weekend, if money allowed, my older brother would escape the farm and take a ride over to Kansas City to see Bernadette. He had stopped bringing me along which made me a little jealous at being left behind. In a day or two he would return with the happiest demeanor, talking at great length about how Bernadette had ambitions of becoming a secretary. She only had to complete her schooling and then she'd have a job with the newspaper lined up and everything. He was thrilled to be dating her and talked excessively about a house he wanted to build on a section of the farm in the future, and when he might get married. His joyfulness spilled out so much at one time that he didn't seem the same guy that I had known my whole life.

* * *

One Saturday afternoon our family, and several other families in town, all were invited to an outdoor get-together at the home of our Aunt Lucy as a sort of send-off for Denzil's departure to military training camp where he would be for at least three months. There were long wooden tables with various platters and bowls of food set up between the massive floral arrangements and overly prepped dishes of food. It all looked like a bit too fancy of a spread considering the rustic character of the property and that Denzil was a male. Oil lanterns hung from the undersides of tree branches to provide adequate lighting when evening came and small candles in paper bags lined the walkway leading up to Lucy's house. She was the closest equivalent to a socialite that our little town knew and everyone there seemed delighted to be on the guest list.

Great Uncle Charles was there, adding his jovial presence to the event and laying enough sections of wood paneling on the ground to create a makeshift dance floor with a bit of straw that eventually created a rather fine powder to make for smooth stepping. My Aunt Lucy had pulled out her best linens and real silverware for her guests, quietly instructing me to watch that the silverware didn't wander off because Charles was known to share not only his possessions with others, but those belonging to our family members as well. Wasn't anything that he wouldn't willingly hand over to another person if he felt they had more need for the thing than he did. When we were very young children he had told us many times the Bible story of the widow's mite—how the widow had given her last coin to tithe, knowing there were others more desperately in need than herself. Mother and the old aunts admired him in principle, but in reality he had also given away a few of the family's treasured possessions that had been carried over on the ship to America. Mother adored Uncle Charles the most—had even named one of the twins after him--but everyone kept an eye on his generosity, especially as he grew older.

For some reason on that particular evening, Denzil was foolish enough to bring his out-of-town date, Bernadette, to this party. As he made the rounds, introducing her to everyone we knew and playing the role of a perfect gentleman, who should show up but Oh-Feel-Ya.

Denzil had never officially acknowledged that Ophelia was his girlfriend, but it didn't take long for her to begin questioning the existence of this out-of-town female named Bernadette in a loud way. When the two women were dangerously close to introducing themselves, I tried to help and stepped in, introducing them briefly by first name only. Denzil added insult to the awkwardness of it all by claiming to Bernadette, who was cuddled up in his arms, that Ophelia was actually our cousin. As he said it, I could see the sun setting in Ophelia's baby blue eyes and upon her visits to our farm.

Bernadette seemed to buy the cousin explanation but before anything else could be said, I quickly assumed my brother's usual role with Ophelia, offering to take her for a drive--away from Aunt Lucy's--in our family's truck. It was a memorable night, not only because it was the first time Denzil had allowed me to drive the old blue pickup without him in it, but also because I was having a great time pretending to be enormously interested in everything that Ophelia had to say. I had heard at some time prior that she had commented upon my handsome looks and I saw this as an advantage, even though I was a few years younger than she. All I wanted to do was avoid an inevitable argument between the two girlfriends of my brother.

Later that same evening, I drove Ophelia to a party out in the middle of the woods that was being held by some of my high school classmates. A group of us paired-off couples walked along the moonlit shore of the lake that evening, then sat around a small bonfire sharing stories and smoking cigarettes until it was time to go home. I had almost understood why my brother liked Ophelia— she was nice to look at and, when talking, she often laid her hands around my neck or rubbed my shoulders a bit, in friendship. I didn't dare cross any lines with her though, knowing the unspoken rule about brothers and women.

Immediately upon returning from Army training, Denzil spent all his free evenings out of town seeing his beloved Bernadette. He looked so different now, his head shaved and even the way he stood in blue jeans seemed like he was wearing a uniform, even though he wasn't. In addition to his regular work on the homestead, he did hours upon hours of physical fitness training by himself out in the barn.

I had looked forward to us spending time together before he went away and I began to despise being left alone out at the farmhouse while he was out having fun with Bernadette. I had no transportation of my own and argued that he should at least take me into town and drop me off at a dance hall for an evening, so that I might have a chance to meet a decent girl my age, too. After all, I reasoned, I had always been my brother's backup in case any fighting came his way--not to mention, his best friend. He refused to include me in his plans though, no matter how much I argued for it. Bernadette was becoming a slight problem for me. The thought of our revelries being usurped by the fascinating Kansas City She-Devil grated me the wrong way and I let him know it; however none of this mattered to him. He told me that when I met someone special I would understand why it had to be like this, but I couldn't imagine being so attached to a woman that I would neglect time with my own brother. We had been inseparable siblings since the day I was born. Now that I was old enough to shave and to drive, I should have been considered his best friend too.

Then, like a miracle, something happened between Denzil and Bernadette. He returned home one evening real late and that next morning barely spoke to anyone at the breakfast table. He became so extra busy around the farm that there was hardly anything left for me to do. I knew he was working out something in his mind, so I didn't try to pry any details out of him in the beginning.

Several days later after the distance between us was growing too much, I ventured into his personal realm. He was out by the old red iron water pump, spreading rocks around the concrete pad. Even though we were living in the middle of nowhere, Denzil was constantly looking for ways to make the property look better. I waited for him to finish then asked him simply, "S-o-o,

Denzil? What happened with Bernadette? Are you split up for good?"

"Seems that way," he said. "Yeah; it's for sure over. Guess you noticed that I haven't been quite right after her and for that, I'm sorry. But you understand that I'm just trying to get myself back into the routine around here before I get sent off to the war anyway?" He handed me his shovel and I leaned on it.

"I can see that, but hell; it doesn't matter to me if you're not yourself right now," I said. God only knows the thoughts you must have going off to war. But as far as Bernadette I suppose it isn't exactly my business is it?" I asked, still wanting to know what happened.

Bending over to rearrange a couple of rocks, then shuffling his foot around in the dirt, he answered. "No, not directly." He looked down and I could tell he was avoiding me staring at him, so I eased off a bit. Then he brushed his hand in the air as if to rid himself of thinking about her. "I let myself get too distracted in that one," he said.

What I couldn't admit out loud was that there was an immense fluttering of happiness in my heart over getting my brother back again. Of course, I didn't want him to feel brokenhearted but I figured that part would just take a little time. "Well," I reasoned. "She was awful special, it seemed to me. Had some nice looks about her. You'd probably have to worry about the other guys stealing her away all the time, anyway. I guess I'd be a mess too, if I had to give up a girl like that."

Denzil looked at me strange for a moment. "You never did know the right thing to say and when," he said, shaking his head. "You're supposed to say something to make me feel better, not make me seem like the loser here."

"Sorry," I said, now fearing to say anything at all. "But don't forget you've always got Oh-Feel-Ya." I sang her name in the same old silly way as I had always said it, then launched into whatever lines from our made-up songs that I could remember from when Denzil and she were so hot for each other. In an instant, I was left standing by myself.

Some evenings later, we ended up driving over to the popular pub in town where we used to meet up with friends. Denzil was sure that Ophelia would be there--

that he could manage to patch things up with her--maybe take up where they left off. We weren't there for but an hour or so before she walked in and, spotting Denzil right away, breezed right past him pretty-as-you-please wearing a strong new perfume and looking much better than I had remembered. Of course, Denzil followed in the same way that a fox follows a rabbit down a trail: head down and tracking her. Me and one of the guys slowly followed them too.

"I'm back on the menu," Denzil announced when she finally stood in one place. I was flanking his right while our friend stood at his left.

She looked down at her freshly manicured hands, toying with the shiny pink polish a little. "Really? And what does that mean to me?"

"Well, it means, if you're interested, you and I can have plenty more happy times together," Denzil said. Then he leaned in towards her and added with his trademark wide smirk, real quietly, "I've missed holding your soft body." The usual hoots of me and his friends were suppressed, waiting to see how this would end.

Ophelia stamped her foot, shifting her weight right and then left, like a horse does when it doesn't want to be moved from one paddock to another. When she looked back at him, I swear I saw her nostrils flare. "I don't see how you're going to be holding my soft body," she said, purposely raising her voice because all of us standing around were tuned-in. "Since I wouldn't dream of having sex with a man who is 'actually' my cousin!" She stared cold into his eyes.

"You can't still be angry with me about that," my brother reasoned.

Ophelia just glared disdainfully at him before moving toward the farthest, darkest wall of the pub. I never saw her look back to check if he was going to pursue her. He watched her go and hung his head for a moment as if recovering from a blow to his person. Instinctively, we all bought a round of drinks and launched into our usual manly conversations and exaggerated story-telling.

It was on that same night that we met two men at the bar that night who were needy beyond belief. They had a hard-luck story to tell and I was just about to run them off when Denzil sat down with them, listening intently.

"Here we go again," I said to our friends. I positioned myself on the outskirts of the conversation because I didn't want to get involved.

"We found a place to get food for a while," I heard the skinny one saying, "so we're covered there. But is it possible one of you fellows knows a good dentist in town?"

"Can't say that I do," Denzil said. "You got some teeth needing fixing?"

It was then that the skinny one smiled and I could see that he had no teeth at all, top or bottom. I tried desperately to hide the expression that was creeping across my face because I didn't want to make him feel even worse by being shocked. Of course, having no teeth at all was an enormous problem, but it wasn't our problem. However; Denzil as always, ventured outside his own realm of possibilities. "Let me think on this seriously," he told the man. I had heard this kind of sincerity in my brother's voice before and I knew that he would think on it because that's the kind of man he was. "Take this pencil here and write down the telephone where I can contact you," Denzil said. He fished a stubby pencil out of his pocket, handed it to the man and turned our bar receipt over for the man to write on it.

"It isn't my number," the man said as he scribbled out a number. "But the landlord who answers this telephone knows where to find me."

Then the skinny fellow's friend stepped up to our table and grinned open-mouthed to show that he also had no teeth. It was then that all of us gasped collectively. "I said I'd see what I could do," Denzil back-stepped, maybe realizing for the first time that it was a tall challenge for him. "I didn't say I could help both of you. I just said I'd try."

"That's enough for us. Thank ya', kind buddy," the skinny one said. They both tipped their caps to us and moved off into the crowd.

"What could we possibly do for them?" I ribbed my brother. "You should've thought about what you were saying with that. Now if we ever see them again, they're going to keep bugging us until you solve a problem which is clearly theirs alone."

"I gave my word only that I would try. That's all," Denzil said. "Maybe I'll try to find a dentist in town to help them. I don't know."

"Let's make 'em some wooden teeth like George Washington had," our friend offered.

But Denzil was no longer listening to either of us. He was watching Ophelia dance with another guy and looking away again before any of us noticed.

After some time, our friend patted Denzil on the back and said, "Hey; forget about that girl. You'll get over her."

"I don't think Ophelia is who's bringing him down," I added. "More than likely he's missing that Bernadette. She's the one he loved the most."

"Neither one is nothing to bring me down," Denzil said. "These things come and go. It's just the way of the corn."

"You're one of the strangest guys I ever met," our friend laughed.

"You have no idea how right you are," Denzil said.

The thought crossed my mind to ask my brother to explain himself, but I wanted him to think that I was maturing enough to begin understanding the ways of the world. I wanted him to see me as more his equal, even though I knew I had a long way to go.

CHAPTER FOUR

One morning, after nearly a week of three of us brothers--Denzil, Auguste and I--setting limestone walls across the entrance to the neighbor's farm to earn some extra money; we decided to take a break. We had been paid and Denzil held the pocket full of money for the three of us before we would return home and divvy it up.

We had driven to a spot almost within the city limits where the riverbank narrowed considerably and slowed its pace. I never knew the real name of the section where we were headed, but everyone called it the Black River because just as soon as one rounded the bend where the sunlight ended, the river became something else—something dark and moody. It was a waterway filled with snags of various sorts like driftwood and things that had wandered downstream in the strong current. We piled out of the truck, grabbing a tackle box and our fishing poles as we always did when there was a new body of water to explore.

Denzil pulled out the cash that the farmer had paid us for our work and he handed the entire wad of it over to Auguste. "Here, hold on to this in your pockets in case Marc and I decide to go for a swim."

I eyed the murky, troubled waters and wondered how many people throughout history regretted ever taking a swim in its clutches. Still, I knew that if Denzil went in, I was not going to let him swim alone.

"But what if I want to swim too?" Auguste asked, stuffing the money into his blue jeans pocket.

"You're not going to today," Denzil said. "There can be a strong current here even when it looks smooth on the top. You need to wait until you're a few years older and a stronger swimmer." Auguste made a frump face but seemed to be so happy to have the feeling of holding the big wad of money that he seemed to brush aside the idea.

Eager to find adventure in this new rough country environment, we boldly bolted down the same path, almost racing each other but staying together all the same. There were great spider webs stretching from tree to tree. I caught one across my mouth as we made our way deeper into a copse of cottonwoods. I coughed and turned to spit away from the path so I wouldn't be rude. As I did, my eyes caught the movement of a dark shadow in the trees.

"I think I just saw a panther," I said to my brothers.

"There's no panthers in Kansas," Auguste informed me. "You're starting to get spooked because you believe those silly tall tales of the fishermen around here."

I had only seen panthers in illustrated storybooks, but I knew that I was afraid of them. "It was taller than us," I said, enhancing so that they would be afraid too.

"Well, maybe it was a damn bear then," Denzil said, obviously enjoying the fact that I was nervous.

We continued ambling around the riverbank on foot, half exploring the woods bordering the river and, since we had our fishing poles with us, halfway fishing for bass. This was a place that I didn't get to visit often, but I loved it from the deepest place in my heart. The ground there was lush with dark green grass, not like the open stretches of mud or dry dirt that covered over half of the county. Here, there were impressive trees--giant maples with leaves as big as your hand and oaks standing in circular formations like ancient guardians of the adjoining hillside. The river water originated from an enormous reservoir many miles away and although it was calm today, at other times of the year when the snow began to melt off, it could become chaotically swollen. Things often floated by in its churning grip, never to be seen again or sometimes, pieces and parts of floaters would get caught in the bushes there. It was also an area known to be frequented by troublemakers and an area that our mother had warned us to avoid, so naturally we wanted to study the place. I hoped every time we went that I might be fortunate enough to stumble upon a wayward ghosted boat that I could restore and use for my own.

We hadn't been at the riverbank for long when we happened upon a bunch of clothes lying on the ground out in the sun. Naturally, we inspected them realizing they were both male and female clothing. Then we turned toward the sound of a group of guys and young ladies about our age, skinny-dipping in the shallow inlet where the thin part of the river met up with a larger channel. They were laughing and splashing about as if they were a world away from civilization. Instantly, Denzil and I recognized two of the guys as a couple of the meanest guys we ever knew in high school. It was the Mazur brothers again.

Their father had recently been in the running to be elected as the county sheriff, and he had promised that if he were chosen, that he would rule the position with an iron fist. As his sons, they were every bit as nasty and vicious as their old man.

The oldest one surely still had a humiliating memory of the kick to the groin he had taken from me. I was guessing that the incident remained only between himself and his brother, as it had with Denzil and I. Between the fist-fights in school and that more recent happening, there was plenty of history of bad blood between us. I wasn't going to let any of it go, so I was quite amused at getting the chance to hit them back for our side.

Without hesitation, I began to gather up the piles of clothing that belonged to the brothers and to throw them into the river, one piece at a time. I left the girl's clothes in place.

"Let those stupid bastards walk home naked," I said, laughing while watching the river carry their clothes downstream.

"Look! Their pants are floatin' just past where they're at," Denzil said, standing several feet behind me and shaking his head incredulously. "They're gonna' be pissed!"

I danced around with delight as the clothes sailed past the spot where the Mazur brothers were swimming.

Someone in the group pointed a finger in our general direction and began waving their arms. They yelled out something inaudible to us before the lot of them scrambled up the riverbank like a herd of naked otters.

"Lemon Suckers!" I yelled out, waving my arms in delight.

"Keep yourself down," Denzil said. "You needn't announce it was us who did this. Now we'd better make a run for it!" We all turned at once to run.

But before we could get even five feet away a big muscled guy, who was much older than any of us, had slipped up behind me. He pressed a rather large pocket knife lying flat up to the side of my face. "You're a tough guy now?" he asked me. I could smell his muskiness, like that of a milk cow.

"No, I'm not." I said, distraught and confused with fear. "I'm sorry for what I did. It's just....we don't like your friends over there." I stared over at my brothers who had stopped, frozen in place.

"Isn't my friends clothes you just dumped in the river," he said tightening his grip on me and backing the both of us away from my brothers. "I'm no part in this. I'm only needin' a little money, alright? Give me your money."

"Shit," I said aloud. I was being robbed. *How could two things so unrelated be happening at exactly the same time?*

"Don't you hurt my brother!" Denzil growled in a voice that I had never heard before. "You hurt him--I swear--I'll hunt you down and kill you with my bare hands!"

Before he even finished the sentence, my younger brother Auguste had already fished into his pockets and was throwing all our money onto the ground towards the man as if we hadn't done an entire week of work to earn it. The big brute released me to grab up the money, still holding the knife straight up towards the three of us. I could see Denzil calculating if he should tackle him and then think better of it. I nearly collapsed to the ground from the shaking in my legs as the robber dashed into the woods and disappeared.

Denzil snatched me up by the shoulders and began shoving me towards the path that led back to our truck. When we looked behind us, we saw the naked Mazur brothers and their girlfriends approaching the place where we had been robbed only seconds ago. I continued running, hyperventilating from everything that had happened. Auguste was crying. Denzil was running ahead, looking over his shoulder, waving me onward. We reached the truck and packed into the front seat in a tight heap as Denzil steered through the trees. He shifted through the gears like a madman until we were completely out of sight of the Mazur brothers.

"That was stupid of us," he said after we had reached the main road. "Why'd you think we needed to do that, Marc? See what happens? Just like Mother warned us about that place. One minute of us not paying attention...look what was there in those woods."

"Think he was an escaped convict or something?" Auguste asked.

"He was a man desperate for money. We've seen a lot of his kind, especially in town, haven't we, Marc?"

"Whoever he was," I said. "I don't care. He can have our damn money. Bastard nearly sliced my throat! Never even got a decent look at him to report it."

"Think about what you just said. We can't go to the police," Auguste reasoned. "Look what we were doing there. We'd better hope that the police don't hear about what we just did too."

"What we did wasn't exactly right but it wasn't criminal either," I defended, talking at the same time as Auguste. "We need to tell the police about that man. He's going to be a threat in those woods again to someone."

Denzil shouted over us. "We're not telling anyone! Furthermore; we've probably got trouble coming our way from the Mazurs after this too."

"I don't care. It was funny as all hell," I said. "I've taken enough bloody noses from those two to enjoy every minute of seeing their naked butts left behind in the woods."

"Can't you just see them driving home naked, dropping those girls off somewhere or having to explain that to their families. They aren't going to ever forget that," Denzil said.

"I do feel kinda' bad for the girls," Auguste said, giggling so much he could hardly speak. "But that's a chance you take skinny-dippin' in the river."

After a few minutes of silence Denzil shook his head, "I actually feel really awful for those girls," he said.

While the truck bounced down the haphazard network of dirt roads towards home, we each tried to put on our seriously remorseful faces while inside I also knew that we were feeling, collectively and mischievously, triumphant.

At breakfast the next morning, I walked downstairs to the kitchen where Auguste was helping our mother with the cooking. I heard him say, "I was there but I want you to know it wasn't me who made the decision to take their clothes. Wasn't me who made the decision to be in those dark woods anyway. I knew what people said about thieves and such being seen around there. I don't understand why Denzil didn't fight him anyway since he's actually trained to fight. Marc could have been killed by that guy."

I had no choice but to face up to it. "No; he's right," I said as I stood in the doorway. "It was me who got carried away, trying to even up with the brothers for the bloody noses we got from them at school. I made the decision to do it. Denzil didn't fight the guy who robbed us because he didn't want to stick around for those brothers to catch up. We would've have more problems. It was the right decision." I was truly annoyed at Auguste for his big mouth, but if I were going to be a real man, I needed to stop blaming my mistakes on my older brother.

"The brothers and paybacks for bloody noses?" Mother implored. "So there's even more besides a man with a knife to your face trying to rob you?" She folded her hands and gave a look up to the ceiling as if asking God to intervene.

"Oops," I said. "Guess he hadn't told you the rest of it, then?"

She shook her head, clearly disgusted with us now, and turned back to the stovetop to whatever she had been cooking. She dismissed us from the room with a wave of her hand over her shoulder. "I don't want to know the rest of it. Please spare me the entire story. I hope you've learned from this dangerous lesson then," she said in a more simplistic tone than usual. I could tell that the angst from us made her tired these days. She turned back to look at us as we walked away, the disappointment showing all over her face. She pointed the wooden spoon at us as she spoke. "There doesn't seem to be anything I say to you boys that keeps you from situations like this. Is this what I can expect from you boys for the rest of my life? One risky thing after another—a steady stream of ignorance from my own children?"

These were the type of questions that we didn't dare to answer until she was finished speaking, if at all.

"Didn't I raise you to think before you act upon every impulse that comes to your mind?" Her voice was shriller now, more desperate. I could see storms gathering in her head. "Why don't you, any of you, ever think about what could happen before you make decisions?" she prodded. "Don't you see that I'm already hurting to have to worry about Denzil having to go off to war?"

I stood there numb, saying nothing. What could I ever say to defend any of our careless actions?

"Answer me!" she shouted and then the rain welled up in her eyes and fell down. They were the tears that carried my mother's unfulfilled hopes for our futures.

I could have beaten the stuffing out of my younger brother for opening his big mouth, but in another way, I was relieved that the truth came out because it forced me to think about my actions. "I can't answer why we do these stupid things all the time," I said, grabbing a handful of biscuits and exiting towards the front door. "But I'm going to try to change, Mother. I promise I'll try."

The long day in the field was an opportunity to be alone and think about where I was headed in this life. I wanted to change, but I simply didn't know how. If I were going to be honest, I would have to say that I did do whatever came to my mind at any given moment. Thinking about what could happen as a result before every decision would be impossible for me, but I was willing to try.

What we had not realized was that the Mazur brothers were telling a story around that same time, to their parents about everything that had happened. Rather than their families demanding more responsibility from their children in their youth as our mother had, their family became inextricably enraged at the events of that day. It was on that day that the whole lot of them had vowed to one day get even with us.

CHAPTER FIVE

My mother's uncle--our great Uncle Charles--was dying. However; he could still carry on a conversation as sharp-witted as anyone and could wholeheartedly muster his trademark booming laugh, although it had quieted down considerably at the end with a cough. Since he had given away nearly everything he owned, his final care fell upon our household. We loved him dearly though so none of us minded.

Now, as he lay abed, lingering in only a body of skin and bones with no luster, his hair practically falling out in patches and his false teeth sitting in a glass of water on the bedside table, we witnessed for the first time in our young lives the trials of a man growing old and the agony of disease. Charles was dying from a liver disease that had turned his skin an odd brownish color. The white part of his eyes had become a dull vapid yellow. I enjoyed talking with him during that time because I was amazed at how, even with all that he was facing up to; he still had a positive outlook and his mind was still like quicksilver for conversation. In typical Uncle Charles fashion, he threatened all of us children that if we didn't mind our parents once he departed from this earth, that he would come back as a ghost and haunt us. Denzil laughed about it like everyone else, but the thought of his threat actually happening frightened me to no end.

We all took turns making visits to comfort him in these last days. We would read books aloud to him, especially the Bible, and feed him bits of oatmeal from a spoon because that was the easiest thing for him to manage to eat.

Finally, when he was no more than a skeleton of about ninety pounds, he passed on to heaven. Father and mother had arranged to hold a wake in the formal parlor room at the front of the farmhouse. Whatever our family owned to be proud of as far as possessions, was displayed with unabashed pride in that room. There was a marble clock from the 1800's on the fireplace mantle, various photographs in frames of family members in France, a bookcase filled with an entire leather-bound encyclopedia set, medical journals (which we had referred to often in our remote location) and various fine china pieces that belonged to Mother and her sisters. The room had always been strictly off-limits to anyone without asking permission first, except for on the occasion of deaths or marriages.

On the day of the wake, I lit the tall beeswax candles and carried several garish floral arrangements as big as a table that had been delivered, helping my mother wherever I could, while my brothers and sisters prepared food platters and scrounged up extra seating from every room in the house. The ensuing viewing service lasted several hours and I realized that Charles was beloved by more people than we expected. Nearly a hundred people passed through the door of our farmhouse that day to pay their respects.

After the crowd had dwindled to four or five people, and then they were all gone, our immediate family members went straight away upstairs for the evening--except for Denzil. Mother had left him as her appointed person to await the arrival of the appointed man who would take Charles' body away to the funeral home. I had volunteered to sit in the parlor and wait too, but Denzil insisted that the duty would be his alone.

Later, after aimlessly wandering around my bedroom for a while, I couldn't resist treading back down the stairs, knowing my brother was sitting there, with only the corpse of our great uncle and himself in the lamplight, waiting for the funeral director's car to arrive. As much as I didn't really want to see the dead body again, as this sort of thing gave me the creeps, I didn't like being excluded from important family matters. It was important to me to share Denzil's sense of duty and be just as much a part of taking care of things as he was. As I rounded the corner to the front parlor, I saw two men in the shadows talking with my brother. Curious at first and then moving in closer, I recognized them as the toothless hard-luck stories from the bar on the night when we had seen the last of Ophelia.

Denzil spied me and lifted a quieting finger up to his lips. He walked over to the coffin, removed the false teeth from Uncle Charles' face, wiped them off with a wet handkerchief and handed them over to the skinny one who popped them into his mouth. After chewing up and down on them a bit, the skinny man passed the teeth to his friend who followed the same path. It was agreed that the teeth were a better fit for the skinny man and, after shaking hands with my brother, they were very quietly escorted outside to a waiting vehicle. Even though Denzil had glanced over and saw me standing there, he said nothing and I remained frozen in place. When my brother returned to the parlor, he ordered me to go to bed and to never speak of what I saw. I didn't know whether to puke or to scream out in protest, but I knew if I did either that Denzil would knock me silly.

During the final church funeral service the next day, with the casket sitting front and center in the aisle of the Lutheran church, I couldn't shake a nagging dread that the mouth of the corpse would fall open and everyone would notice the blatant emptiness. Denzil sensed that I was uptight about it and just to rile me further, belted out a perfect copy of one of Uncle Charles' great booming laughs in the middle of the sermon. When several people turned to look at us, Denzil remarked, "Can't you just hear him laughing right now?" and nudged me with his elbow as part of our inside joke.

"I don't see a damn thing funny about it, Denzil," I said in a low voice so that only he and I could hear. I was genuinely upset with him, although he didn't seem to care. "Don't make light of such a thing in the church," I said.

He whispered back to me out of the side of his mouth. "You may not realize it but you just swore in the church. I'd think that's worse. Besides, he's not needing those teeth where he's gone now, Marc. Settle yourself and try to carry on like a normal person. Your eyes look befuddled--like those of a chicken tangled in a net. People are staring at you."

I looked around me and several members of the congregation were staring. Of course, he was right, but the incident from the night before still left me feeling more than a little unhinged. Right up until the end of our life together I never again, even once saw those two men again, nor did I bring up this subject to Denzil. It was something I simply couldn't bring myself to dig up again.

* * *

All at once; it was time. My oldest brother, my best friend, was really preparing to go off to fight in World War II. He had never traveled outside of our state and now he would be headed to Europe under the worst possible scenario imaginable. I was shocked it was actually happening and yet proud of the way Denzil was facing his deployment as a true American patriot. I didn't really know anyone who had shipped out to war, so the overall emotional effect was new territory for me. No doubt, my life would change in his absence and I struggled against the selfishness of feeling sorry for myself. It wasn't until he had actually left us that a heavy dread fell over me as I began to consider how being sent to war might impact his life.

"What do you think it will be like?" I had asked him. "Do you really feel like you're adequately prepared to go?"

"Of course I am," he replied. "Every soldier who's shipping out is a hundred percent ready. We've spend months training, marching, loading and unloading and cleaning our weapons. I'm as physically fit as the next soldier and just as determined that we will win this war," Denzil said.

"What if you don't know what to do when it gets really terrible?" I shouldn't have asked this, but my heart was in a rather panicky state at this point.

"Listen, Marc; all I know is that as long as I follow orders and pay attention to everything, not making mistakes, I'm going to be okay. God will protect me, not because I deserve it, but because he knows that I need to come back home to our family. And if it does turn out that it is my turn to go, then it would've been my turn to go, whether I was here or over there."

Realizing that I should be sending my brother off on a more positive note, I switched the conversation. "Well, I guess that anyone coming from our state is the best of the best and the enemy doesn't stand a chance of victory," I said, putting extra guts in my voice so he knew I was behind him all the way.

"That's the idea," Denzil said. "Victory at any cost." With that, he hitched his duffel bag up onto his shoulders and headed down the stairs.

I wouldn't see him again for several years and at that moment, I wasn't sure if I would ever see him again at all.

* * *

My father had always been a rather cantankerous man who offered few words to conversations and a displayed a short temper when things didn't go according to his plan. When my own draft papers arrived a short time after Denzil shipped out, Father had spared me by driving into town one day and pointing out to the powers-that-be (as he called them) that I was at that time, the only remaining male left who was able to help with the family's farm. How he did this with Auguste and Samuel and Charles and Cain, four boys total, still living at home, was beyond me. I had no urge to trek through foreign lands lugging a gun and fighting for my life anyway. I'm truly ashamed now, as an older man, to admit that I didn't object to his interference.

Losing Denzil as his most competent and reliable son had given Father quite a jolt to our family's sense of security. He took to drinking a lot more in the evenings soon after Denzil left. The fear of losing any of his remaining sons to the war effort had driven him to grasp for some loophole to excuse me from service, but in the privacy of our home—to me—he had outright stated that I wasn't made of the right stuff for military service. "You're slow in the head and weak in the guts," he said once to me when he was drinking.

In my younger years I had never measured up to his expectations and now that he was growing older, he became crankier, more disappointed in all of us, including mother. Making mean-spirited statements aloud to any of us seemed to have become much easier to him as the years progressed. Knowing that what he said about me was probably true, didn't keep it from hurting my pride all the same. Inside myself I wanted to be a fighter, a wolf, a brave young man, but on the outside the fear of the war had me falling apart. I didn't have the right stuff to take up arms for a cause in a foreign land. Unless someone invaded our house and I needed to defend our family, I saw no need for it. It had always been my oldest brother who had never faltered in the face of conflict. He was the one who had always felt the urge to defend the helpless, not me.

Father usually laid down instructions to me each morning over the breakfast table. He outlined his objectives for the homestead to me as if I were just another farmhand, not as if I were an important member of the family. It was as if, in his eyes, I could never shake the laziness of my youth or prove myself capable no matter how hard I tried. Mother usually sat nearby, hearing everything, but never saying a word towards my defense. During those days, she had become somewhat detached to anything that might add to a conflict or upset the household.

One morning, during my father's daily breakfast review he said to me, "You need to take up your older brother's responsibilities around here now a lot more than you're doing. Work the farm as if it were your own. It'll be yours one day if your brother doesn't make it through the war, you know."

Suddenly, inside me a fire smoldered. I couldn't believe our own father would say such a thing to me. To even suggest that Denzil wouldn't return sent a burning pain through the front of my skull. I jumped to my feet. "Denzil's a natural born fighter," I said with angry certainty as I banged my fist on the long wooden table. "He's the best fighter, the fastest runner in this whole town and has powers of observation that nobody else in this family has." It was my left-handed way of including my father in the 'not-so-smart' category too.

"I've never seen any man able to outrun bullets and bombs yet," Father said in his usual sarcastic voice of authority. It was doubly insensitive too, that he had said this in front of our mother who then began to cry.

"Denzil's coming back and now I'm leaving!" I shouted, leaving the breakfast table and kicking the bottom of the wooden screened front door where it always stuck. It swung open and I made sure to let it go with the spring fully extended so that it would slam loudly behind me. I knew that was something that irritated the shit out of him. At that moment, I made up my mind that not only would I continue to take over my brother's role on our family's farm, but I would learn whatever I didn't already know about how to run an agricultural business. I walked deep into the woods where I sat for a few hours just to clear my thoughts at my favorite get-away spot.

While I was growing up, I knew that my father had been disappointed in almost everything I did and now the childhood memory of how he had often struck me with the short leather strap kept close by his reclining chair, stung my very being. Now that I was almost six feet tall, he had ceased physically striking me, choosing instead to discipline me with cutting words. It never crossed my mind to show any physical aggression toward him out of respect, but I had taken note that the balance of power in the household was shifting ever-so-slightly. The only way he could penetrate my young man's bravado now was to point out my inadequacies and I wasn't about to let him beat me down.

As the evening was falling, I wandered back up towards the house and as I approached I could see a flurry of activity out on the front porch. In the shifting winds, I could also smell chicken frying so I quickened my pace home.

My three sisters were bustling about trying to be cheerier than usual and carrying various dishes from the kitchen to the outside. "Sorry for running out on everyone," I said to my sisters, as I approached. "I should've been here to help, but I didn't realize the time."

"Sure you didn't. Grab a plate," my youngest sister, Marne yelled out to me. "We're eating on the porch tonight."

"I see that," I said wondering what the occasion might be. "Where's mother?"

"In her bedroom, last I knew," my big sister Lucy said, adding quickly, "Uh, you might want to just stay down here. She's kind of got the blues due to Denzil being gone and everything."

"Uh, no," I said in the same voice she had given me. "I'm going to go up and see her then."

When I walked into the bedroom, I saw the pair of porcelain praying hands on mother's nightstand that were lighted up from a tiny bulb inside. "You praying?" I asked, opening the door slightly.

"Come on in," she said. "I'm finished. Are you ready for a big supper? We've cooked enough for twenty people it seems."

I saw then that she had been crying and I rushed to console her. "Mother, it's alright. I'm so sorry for running off in anger like that. Father makes me so mad, but I didn't know I'd make you upset like this."

"It's that, Marc and my worries about Denzil, too. I couldn't bear to lose any of my children. I love each one of you so much."

"We're all feeling the weight of worry about Denzil. Father shouldn't have suggested any chance of him not coming back. That's what's upsetting you, isn't it?"

"That--and also that he's my first child to leave home. Having eight more really doesn't make the pain of that any more bearable as you might think it would. I'll be a complete mess if I lose any of you."

"You're not going to," I said with a new determination in my voice. "Please stop saying that. I'm taking care of things while Denzil's gone. I know you haven't always seen the best side of me, but believe me; I'm capable of doing this. I'm capable of rising up to whatever challenges are coming our way. And Father will see that too, in time. I'm going to prove to him and everyone else in this county, that I'm not the blatant fool I've shown myself to be in the past."

She placed her hand alongside my cheek, as she used to do when I was a young boy. Only this time, I know she felt the rough beard that told her I was now a man. "You're young, Marc," she said, looking into my eyes. "We're all fools when we're young. And some of us remain fools even when we're older. We battle within ourselves between the good memories and the bad memories. Mothers will just be sentimental now and then." She brushed her long brown hair back from her face, tucking it on both sides behind her ears and straightened her posture. "Let's get downstairs then and have a nice supper all of us, alright?"

I walked with her arm-in-arm downstairs in a deliberately foolish Charlie Chaplin way to make her laugh and we strolled out onto the porch together where everyone was waiting.

"Anything wrong?" Marne asked.

"Yes," I said looking at the long table of food platters. "I think we're going to be needing more biscuits."

We all bowed our heads as Father said the prayer, and as if to soften what he had said earlier, he put in an extra request to God. "Keep Denzil safe and bring him home in one piece."

I cringed at his choice of words, saying nothing, and the rest of those seated at the table breathed a collective, "Amen!"

CHAPTER SIX

The late afternoon sky was a hazy green-purple and a wall of rain illuminated the dark distant horizon with each flash of lightning. A couple of our hound dogs had begun to bark non-stop and our smallest dog was whimpering. The other farm animals appeared restless in their pens. Without even speaking, all of our family had gathered in the front yard for a better view of the sky. When the neighbors living nearest to our homestead drove up the driveway in their family car, they came with a warning about what we had already suspected. Tornadoes had been spotted several miles down the road and they seemed to be headed in the same direction as our farm. The neighbors had used the mere minutes available to warn each household to be ready. They didn't stop to make conversation about the weather; they were gone as quickly as they arrived.

Our entire family knew the drill, for we had practiced scenarios like this on the day of the summer solstice every year, as a tradition. The whole lot of us ran the nearly eighty feet from the front of the house towards the safety of the underground storm shelter. I was the first one to reach the metal door and I swung it open and let it drop to the ground while everyone lined up. I looked up at the sky again, horrified after taking note of how quickly the landscape was changing, how quickly the skies were turning an ominous grey-green.

"Is it going to be bad?" my little sister Odette asked as she waited for father to catch up to us. "Will it take away our whole house and everything?" I could see the fear in her eyes as she clutched her handmade cloth dolly by its arm. Charles and Cain rushed ahead of her and scrambled down the steps first as if it were all a new adventure.

Father scooped Odette up with his strong hands and placed her on his back. "Don't worry, Little One. I've gotcha'," he said with a healthy measure of cheer.

Her small arms held on tight around his neck.

"Hold on," he said. "We've got to get down these steep stairs safely. After that, we just wait." There was a gentleness in his voice that would have calmed me too, if I hadn't realized that it was actually masking his own fear. Odette looked the doll squarely in the face and tried to manage a smile for it.

Mother followed next, holding onto Marne's hand as she treaded each step individually, for she was the most timid--next to Odette. "Don't worry about the future right now, if this turns out for the worst. For certain it would make our lives more difficult for a time before we could rebuild," she told us collectively as we jostled in the darkness to find the flashlights and blankets. "But for certain also, if the worst does happen, we'd have the help of many people around town."

As more of us filed down the stairs and moved toward the back, we formed a circle around the edges of the concrete room, sitting on the wooden benches. Mother, with Marne seated on her lap, kept talking nervously while keeping one eye on the door that was still open. I wasn't sure if her somewhat random chatter was an attempt to console herself or us. "When I came to this farm before any of you were born, I knew that I wanted to live my entire life here. It was my idea to buy this farm," she said. "And it wasn't for the house. That original small footprint of a house merely came with the property, but we rebuilt it and added on to it until it was perfect for us. It was the potential of this land I saw—and little at a time we built grain storage silos, reinforced the old barns that were already on the land, and collected the machinery in the shop one piece at a time. No matter what happens I want us to remember that these things can be rebuilt, if necessary. Our determination has kept us going so far, not the other parts of this homestead or even the house itself."

Our father cut in. "Well, that doesn't really matter at this minute. What matters is that we stay down here until the storm has passed. Then we'll be alright." It occurred to me that in some way our mother had been more enthusiastic about the farming life from the beginning than he ever was. Overall, she had always seemed to relish the idea of not knowing what the next seasons of rough weather or droughts might bring. The challenges were only part of this life the way she looked at it, but why she needed to tell us all about it at that very moment was beyond me.

The winds above our concrete storm shelter picked up substantially as Father began to climb the stairs to close the door. He called each child's name out, quickly accounting for us. Then he said, rather panicky, "My

God! Samuel and Auguste still aren't here!" He darted up the stairs again and disappeared into the growing blackness.

After a long minute or so, all three; father, Auguste and Samuel, appeared at the top of the stairs. I moved to help Samuel, with his polio-damaged legs, maneuver down the steep wooden stairs. Then, Auguste, after lowering a makeshift wooden ramp over the stairs, dragged a stinking pregnant cow down there with us, followed by a couple of baby pigs and a pair of bewildered chickens.

"Are you Noah?" Lucy chided him. "Not only should we be packed in here uncomfortably with ten people but we should suffer the stink of the animals brought in two-by-two, also?"

"You'll thank me if everything is lost within the next hour," Auguste answered, shoving the ramp back outside of the door and securing it closed with the steel pin latch. He was a teenager now, the age where he was trying to prove his mettle just as I had done only a few years before.

"That was stupid," I said. "Now when the wind blows your ramp away, how will we get these animals up out of here again? You never think things through all the way do you?" I was rather relishing taking him to task as my older brother had often done with me.

"Quiet kids!" Mother whispered loudly. "Listen to the wind as it passes. Stay alert and be prepared for whatever you might see after we emerge from this awful hole."

Odette couldn't be silent. She was what my Aunt Claudette used to call a 'Sensitive', meaning a person who picked up on the vibrations of things that ordinary people didn't see or feel. "I've got the creeps down here," she whined looking all around. "It stinks and it feels like there's a ghost crawling all over on my skin. I can feel it all around me. It's making my neck feel cold."

Everyone remained silent as if she had said nothing.

"I mean it," she tried again. "There's ghosts in here crawling on my skin, giving me chills!"

Lucy grabbed Odette's dolly from her and floated it over her head. "Ghosts don't crawl on your skin. They just float over you and bite your head clean off!" Lucy said, barking out like a dog and snort-laughing seeing Odette getting more scared.

"Shut up about the ghosts," Mother said, snatching the doll out of Lucy's hands. She put her hand momentarily over Odette's mouth. "If you say it again, I'm going to smack you." Odette had never been slapped before and just the fact that our mother had threatened it, made everyone in the storm shelter instantly quiet.

Odette took her doll back, clutching it to her heart, and remained still as the hail began to fall. Within seconds, it was banging against the thick metal door overhead like a hundred hammers.

"I hope the tornado doesn't take away our house," Cain said.

"Me too," Charles agreed. "I hope it turns around and goes the other way." The twins had found a blanket to wrap around themselves and were huddled together like two trapped rabbits as the wind howled louder and louder overhead.

The rain began as a treacherous downpour that instantly found the small hole in the door, leaking in a steady drip into the crowded space. There was plenty of lighting flashing through the edges too and the strikes must have been nearby because the ground vibrated with every bolt. We sat there, all ten of us, a pregnant cow, a pair of pigs and a couple of chickens in very tight quarters, enduring the heavy storm. All at once, a roaring rumbling monster moved across the ground above us like nothing I had ever heard. I had heard people describe tornadoes as if they made the sound of a train, but I remember thinking that it sounded like something that was alive yet screaming in agony. Inside of me I wanted to cry but if I did, I knew that everyone down in that concrete hole in the ground would have been crying too. The thought of keeping my siblings strong until the worst of this situation passed (and remembering that where Denzil was now had to be far worse than any tornado) held my tears back. As the final and worst part of the tornado passed overhead everyone else began crying aloud underneath the roaring sound of it, except for me and Father. Gradually the worst of it was dying down and after some shorter grumbling sounds came and went, the rains continued for at least another twenty minutes or so before an uneasy silence fell over us. All the animals visibly relaxed as if they knew the storm was over. It was now freezing cold and damp from the leaks into the concrete room. It smelled heavily of human sweat and was uncomfortably small to share with the jostling farm animals. Our flashlight was starting to flicker as if it were going to go out.

At last, our parents decided it was safe enough to venture out and Mother climbed the stairs, throwing open the metal doors to the still-darkened sky. I supposed we were all imagining the damage we might see when we emerged. One by one each of us emerged and began inspecting the damage. Miraculously and clearly, the storm had not taken away our farmhouse. Maybe it was its destiny to stand there for another hundred years or more. There was a visible path though of a tornado that had destroyed a wide swatch of our biggest trees. "We're going to have a lot of firewood for this winter," I said, trying for optimism.

My brother Auguste was struggling to take the cow back up the small concrete steps and I backtracked in order to help him coax her back home. All of our livestock that had been left behind had miraculously survived the storm, so for that we were grateful.

It's quite funny to me now when I think about it. I can still remember smelling the sweat and dirt from my family members who had already worked so hard in the fields on that morning. I can still remember praying that one of those animals sheltering with us didn't have to poop.

Upon further inspection later, we found that the damage from the tornado had been more extensive than we originally noticed. Still, the farmhouse, though damaged on one corner of the roof and having a few broken windows, had fared rather well. It was as if the winds had plowed straight through a couple of our supply and maintenance buildings while skipping a wide margin around the house. Each one of us set about collecting and salvaging as many of our possessions as possible. Our farm tools and even some of the equipment had been spread far away from the main building where we stored the machinery. Putting everything back in order and rebuilding the damaged maintenance structures took weeks instead of days. Even a year later, we would search for some tool that we knew had once existed only to realize that it had been taken away.

What we had lost surfaced in other places too. After the prior incident with the thieves who had tried to steal our produce, our father had developed the habit of diligently painting our equipment--the handles of our tools and such--with a bright red paint, hand-lettering our family name over the top. Almost ten years after that tornado, a heavy old wood planer was found in a field three miles away; and the farmer who found it on his property made a special trip to drive out to our property to return it.

* * *

During the first year that I was learning to be in charge of running the farming operation, the rainfall had been less than normal. Therefore; the crops were weaker than normal. It seemed the ground was practically eating up fertilizer and the grasshoppers had chewed their way through our acreage like a Biblical plague. When the rains finally came, the frogs and rabbits seemed to come as a deluge out of nowhere, so I learned to deal with both of them. The abundance of frogs was more of a nuisance than anything but the explosion in the rabbit population did so much damage that I had to harvest several of them. I don't remember our family eating rabbits at any time before my sisters joyfully cooked these up, but as it turned out, with the right herbs and under their skillful hands, these were a tasty addition to our dinner table.

Early on in the following season, in addition to our purchased nutrients and naturally composted material, I found a used five-hundred-gallon boom spreader that we could use to more efficiently get the waste of the pigs and cattle out onto the fields. I employed Samuel to drive it which was like an honor to him, since with his slight walking disability, the other tasks of farming were better left to the healthiest of us. He had a fantastic sense of humor and had affixed wooden signs high up on each side of it that, with Father's help, he had painted in big fancy lettering. They read, 'THE HONEY POO WAGON'. It was a delightful reminder of a tradition started by Denzil when he had placed all of his philosophical signs across the eight hundred acres when we were much younger. Because of spreading that stinking honey-poo, our crops yielded at least twenty percent more and the grasshoppers stayed away. Thereafter; we were all very enthusiastic about collecting the effluent from the livestock to keep that sweet fertilizer spread across the topsoil.

CHAPTER SEVEN

The immense workload of the farm that had fallen naturally onto me became heavier than I could have ever imagined. Not only was I managing the daily chores but also the crop sales to the in-town buyers. I had mentored my younger brother Auguste along in the same way that my older brother had done for me. However; Auguste was fairly lazy, more so than I had ever been. As a result, I ended up doing the majority of the more difficult chores myself. I realized through trial and error that my younger brother worked best on one task at a time, not an outlined list of tasks to complete in a day which only served to overwhelm him. I began to notice the way in which every individual on the homestead carried out their tasks and I adjusted the workload to get the most out of each person's level of skill or motivation. As a side effect, our production actually increased.

Naturally, I expected my parents would have made some mention of my renewed efforts for efficiency over a dinner or at least make a comment or two stating that I had successfully taken on Denzil's role, in his absence. I wanted this acknowledgement more than anything. My internal anticipation of being recognized grew to such a level that I was feeling slighted when the praise didn't come. One day I got the courage up to go fishing for compliments from my father.

The family was gathered around the dinner table passing around the various bowls of green beans, potatoes and corn. A large oval platter of roast beef sat near the head of the table where Father always sat. He was carving it up and passing plates as fast as a man could to serve a family of ten, plus my sister Lucy's new husband and baby girl who had been appropriately named Lucy as well.

Lucy's husband, Joe, had grown up in a northeastern American household where fully prepared plates were served to each person. He showed a distinct awkwardness with our traditional passing around of the food bowls and platters to serve oneself. We all enthusiastically encouraged him to keep it moving, as there were always still plenty of chores to finish before we each turned into our rooms for the evening. "Maybe we should start to put the food in the center of the table again instead of passing it," Auguste said, watching Lucy's husband furtively. "Remember the night we had the bowl of biscuits and the lights went out?"

Nobody remembered.

"Yeah," he continued. "Just before it went pitch dark I had reached for a biscuit. When the lights came back on I drew my hand back and it had seven forks in it!"

"Dear God!" Joe gasped. "That must've been painful."

Auguste smirked, proud of himself for delivering a joke with such ease.

Lucy broke out with her trademark snort-laugh which everyone but me thought was atrocious.

"That must've been bullshit. Never happened," Samuel said. Normally he would have been in trouble for swearing, especially at the dinner table, but everyone was laughing so hard they let him get away with it.

I decided to change the subject quickly. "Have all of you noticed the profits have nearly doubled since I've taken over the business side of things for the farm?" I asked, knowing that everyone at the table had seen the ledger because I kept it posted on the wall in the kitchen.

Lucy, missing the point entirely, immediately began begging to be more involved in things, offering to help me with accounting if needed. She had been working part time on weekends at a general hardware store in town and had learned a great deal there about managing money. Father, without acknowledging my question, finally chimed in and coaxed me to agree that she could handle the books, but added that I should still oversee her work. I knew that letting a young woman have all the reins on a family's financial well-being usually wasn't done, even if she was employed in town and married now. Hearing our father support her ambition felt like a positive change for womankind and my sister was beyond excited over the idea. Still, what I was really after was recognition for my own efforts.

My younger brother Auguste finally spoke up about my role in managing the farm. "We oughta' have a few thousand dollars more the way you're breaking my back out there every day. I can't see where we're getting ahead considering all the hours we're working. It's like the day never ends."

"Don't feel sorry for yourself," Father said. "Each one of you enjoys filling your mouths with food then, don't you? If it takes working all day in the hot sun; that's what it takes. Everyone's doing our share around here. It isn't just you, Auguste."

Then I cut in trying again to get back to the subject of my successful management of the farming operation. "Surely you can all see that I'm taking our operations here to a better standing than we've ever seen." I coaxed. "My efforts are helping our whole family to do better and it's only going to keep on being successful. I'll make sure of it." I was blowing my own horn and it felt pretty great.

"So you want us to say that the high numbers this year are all due to your efforts? Is that correct?" my father asked. "Like Lucy, her husband, Samuel, Auguste and even the twins aren't pulling their fair share?"

"Sure, everyone's working. But, yes, the high numbers are due in large part to my extra efforts. Before Denzil left he asked me to make sure we all kept a good life here and I've tried to do that. I've been a more responsible, more thoughtful man, too. I'm really not that rowdy, hell-raiser that I was even two years ago. I'm actually pretty good."

Immediately Father returned, "Well then, what kind of 'good' are you? Would that be 'good for nothing' or 'no good at all'?"

Everyone at the table, except for mother laughed out loud. She gave my father a look that only a husband recognizes as a silent admonishment. He might have been only kidding on the outside, but the truth was that he meant part of it inwardly. I could have let this fill me with anger, but knowing that most of my family members had, at one time of another, viewed me as a sort of half-wit; it only strengthened my resolve to keep going.

It was evident to me that people inside our family felt too comfortable treating me as if I didn't have a sense of business, even when the numbers told otherwise. It was the driving force behind my decision to make myself an educated corn farmer. I began to go into town and borrow books from the state farmer's extension office and the library. I asked for meetings with other farmers who had been in business for longer than we had so that I could glean those important methods and secret techniques that can only come from years of experience. There was so much more to know about farming from a scholarly standpoint, than I ever knew.

With the help of our state office, I also managed to find workers to hire for additional help with the more laborious tasks. Braceros, or Mexican farmhands, would work for fifty dollars a week back then, including the room and board we provided for them in the downstairs back portion of the house. There were three additional bedrooms and a bathroom there and they were a close-knit bunch who didn't mind sharing two or three to each small room. They were strong and willing and had a tremendous willingness to tackle anything that needed to be done. Mother didn't take immediately to the idea of strangers being in our household, but I reassured her that they were just as honorable as anyone we knew locally. There were six of them, all males, and their leader spoke English well enough that I could communicate everything that we needed to do. These enthusiastic migrants worked long hours in the hot stark Kansas sun while never complaining, for their end goal was to return back to their homeland with a hefty amount of money for their wives and children. I had watched their handiness with machetes in the fields and I felt their loyalty to our family provided us with another layer of necessary security considering the unsettling events that continued to happen in town.

Recruiting women from the town to work on the farm proved difficult. Before the war, getting Kansas women to help with various farming chores had been easy. Now, they were able to earn nearly a hundred dollars a week with various jobs in the city which kept us out of the running as employers. It was as if the war had made the female gender more strong-willed than ever. They all seemed to want to be nurses, teachers and secretaries, not farmhands. My little sister, Marne, had become obsessed with the aviation heroine Amelia Earhart and was often lost in a weird daydream of becoming a military bombing pilot. I didn't know what to make of how the war was changing all of us. What I did know for certain was that it was going to be up to me to keep a constantly evolving plan in motion for the survival of our family until its favored eldest son Denzil returned home.

I sincerely missed my brother more each day. His absence had left more than a need for me to step up on the homestead; it was leaving a distressing pain in my heart. His letters that had been frequent in the beginning of his deployment, had dwindled to maybe one or two in a month. He made sure to mention the name of each of our siblings when he wrote which seemed to me like his way of staying connected to them. Mother would trace the lines of ink and even smell the paper sometimes as if there might be a hint of her son's surroundings carried in the envelope over the ocean. I was noticing that she was growing visibly older with each passing month, the grey creeping into her dark brown locks and the brightness fading from her eyes. She was unable to keep up with even the basic house chores, and my father, instead of pitching in to help, was beginning to stay in his living room chair watching television every day after lunchtime.

Although our grain and livestock sales had increased over fifty percent as the war was ending, we still wouldn't make profit enough to keep us through the winter if we started paying wages to employees of either gender that would compete with those paid for jobs in town. It was Mother who eventually came up with a solution to this problem when she recruited two of the old aunts to drive the tractors for half a day each. Aunt Lucy would show up in the morning and do her share then Aunt Claudette would come and eat lunch with us and do her part until it was almost dark. They not only drove the tractors to cultivate the corn, they harvested the corn, de-tasseled it and, when I couldn't get away from the farm, drove the trucks into town to sell the crops. We paid them a small wage and shared dairy and vegetables for their families.

I had become almost as handy as Denzil with regard to the old farm equipment as well as the new machinery we were able to buy. Now, I could fix boilers and pumps and I knew how to take engines apart on any car or farm vehicle and find out what might be keeping it from running right. As with any skill, much of what I learned came from making my share of mistakes and asking others who knew more about equipment than me. Even if I had to stay up in my bedroom late at night studying repair manuals or work out in the barn by the light of a kerosene lantern, tinkering with an idea for a fix; I did it willingly.

The largest of our crops was still corn, but the smaller crops of flax, potatoes, peas and beets were becoming important to the overall operation too. I shuttled truckloads of these into town on a regular basis depending on when they were ready. We put enough produce on reserve for my sisters to either can or put in the root cellar for storage to keep our family fed for the coming winter. In the evenings after dinner, my father would return to the overstuffed living room chair where he would read books or watch television while drinking a glass of whiskey. As hard as I was working to conserve our money, it angered me that he indulged in this luxury for himself. I had to remind myself at times, that he was the actual head of our family and that he had also contributed a great deal to our success, especially when we were only children. I remained fixated on the possibility that I could keep the momentum going and even surpass any accomplishments we had gained so far.

One day I was out in the field talking to the braceros that I had hired. They were a serious bunch and even though almost all of them had learned enough English to communicate well with our family they still kept a certain distance, a certain respectful hierarchy to their demeanor. When I asked them to stop working and speak with me, they simply glanced up from whatever they were doing and appointed one person to walk over to speak with me. The rest of them then immediately went back to work. I knew it was important to discuss our plans with them and I knew, too, that they had communications in town with other migrants and immigrants who had come from the same area of Mexico as they had.

Their designated speaker informed me that down in Texas, some farmers were actually having luck growing cotton. Cotton was a big commodity and as soon as I heard this, I wanted to try my hand at it. When I discussed this exciting possibility with the other local farmers and asked for their help with what I was trying to do, there was open laughter and skepticism, and nobody offered to help me. Later that year, when rumors traveled to town that I was having some success, more than a few of them wandered out to the farm under an assumed reason just to observe the area where I had planted it. Feeling a sort of a pioneer, I sheltered and babied those cotton bushes until I had a bumper crop. No one locally had ever seen or heard of cotton being grown in Kansas. There was a willing group of high school students, boys and girls, who were so enamored with the novelty of it, that they agreed to work for us at a fairly low wage picking it. The ensuing crop brought us an extra thousand dollars that year.

By venturing into new crops my status personally in the agricultural realm had gone up considerably. Our farm that only three years prior had profits of a couple thousand dollars (a generous take back then) was now seeing profits of over ten thousand dollars. While other farmers were barely surviving or just breaking even, our farm was increasing profits every year. When I wasn't farming I was taking classes at the college forty miles away, determined to earn my degree in agriculture.

At the end of that season's harvest period, after all the monies were distributed to the homestead, I drove into town to do some shopping with my share of the profits. I had been frugal and even downright stingy on buying anything for nearly a year and now I was on a mission to spend some money. There were war time posters at many of the public places encouraging all patriotic Americans to conserve supplies and to keep our spirits up. I didn't give these suggestions even a second thought as I purchased for mother a pretty pink linen dress from one of the fancy shops. It was shaped just like the ones that my mean beautiful teacher used to wear. I insisted that the store clerk wrap it up in special paper and add a big yellow bow. When I took it home, Mother unwrapped the gift excitedly, as a child does when receiving a Christmas package. She opened the doors to the parlor and held it up to her body while she stood in front of the long wood framed mirror. There were tears in her eyes when she looked back at me. "Where in the world am I gonna' wear this, Marc?" she asked.

My sister Lucy stood nearby, showing enormous enthusiasm over the dress. It occurred to me that I should have bought one for her too, although I hadn't seen her in a dress since she graduated out of high school. Besides, it appeared to me that she had moved up another size and I wouldn't begin to know how to guess it.

"Drive yourself into town and wear it into the big diner," I said to my mother. "Buy a malted drink and sit with some friends or take Lucy and Odette with you. Sit and talk awhile," I said. "Hell, wear it around the house while you're cooking and cleaning—I don't care. I thought you needed it. You like it; don't you?"

"I love it," she said. "I just love it," she said, beaming with a smile like I had not seen in the past few years. My father started to say something from the other side of the living room, but then threw both his hands up as if realizing that he was outnumbered. I had taken over the household bills and had been running the farm almost completely by myself. While he mostly sat around barking orders from his armchair and watching the television whenever the antenna would let the picture be clear, my mother had been breaking her back with household chores. At the least, she deserved a beautiful dress.

Every month since my brother was drafted into the Army, I had written long newsy letters telling him about all that I was doing on the farm. It had been some time since I had received a reply back from him, but I kept sending my letters anyway. I especially wanted him to know that I was taking good care of our mother, as I knew that would make him happy. It was especially delightful to write a letter to tell him about buying the fancy pink dress. After a month or more of no response, I began to think of the worst kinds of things that might have happened to my brother. Then a letter arrived. He was well and fighting inside Germany itself.

In some way, as much as I hate to admit it, I was grateful for the war keeping my brother away for a while. I was beginning to shine in my own right for things that I never even dreamed of doing while I lived in his shadow. Even though I was a grown man, I still had enough of the naivety that comes with being raised in a rural environment that I wasn't fearful he would be killed. I truly believed if anyone could survive a battle, it would be him. It was due to his absence that I strived to become myself without his direction. As I was growing up, it had been my big brother's initial guidance in our youth that steered many of my decisions—now I was learning that I could figure out life on my own. I had become successful in the farming business, not only by growing corn, but by growing bountiful crops of every kind of vegetable grown in Kansas and even cotton that had not been traditionally grown there, just to see if I could do it.

* * *

Denzil had been away for nearly four years when suddenly he returned without any warning. He just walked up the long dirt driveway, opened the new white picket gate that Auguste and Samuel had recently made, and followed the well-worn path up to the front porch. As he arrived, there were gasps and then shrieks of joy as we all filed out one at a time, our father and mother, then all eight of us siblings in a state of surprise--plus Lucy's husband and baby. There was a jubilant confusion as we led him into the wide open dining room and forcibly seated him into a chair. There were so many outstretched hands rubbing his shoulders and offering hugs. Mother was crying and stroking his hair as if he were one of our barn cats.

I personally took the heavy canvas duffel bags and the rucksack he carried up to his room and placed them on his bed. Not wanting to appear overly sentimental, I fought back my own tears while trying to keep a lid on the fact that I was bursting with happy emotion to see my brother again. However; I do remember actually jumping up and down a couple of times upstairs while there was no one around to see it.

When I returned downstairs to the great celebration that had instantly commenced in the dining room, I saw my brother standing at the center of our world again. The smiles had returned to our parents' faces and the youngest, the twins and my little sister Marne, were running around in circles chasing each other as if their hyper excitement just needed an outlet. Suddenly all manner of things was well again. We then collectively seemed to realize how we had not quieted down to let him speak. It was Father first, who asked Denzil to share with us a light version of what the preceding years had been like for him.

The whole family was gathered around listening to Denzil report on the warfront in a way that none of us had gleaned from the newspapers. It was a shocking review, even the short version.

"And I got shot," I remember him saying at one point. And then, he took open the zipper from his Levi's blue jeans and pulled them down halfway to his thigh, spinning toward the sisters and brothers gathered around. When we saw the wound on the left side of his buttocks just above the leg, long raised scars seemingly pieced and stitched like a quilt, like puzzle pieces lost and then found again, we all shuddered at once. Mother cried aloud when she saw it. Denzil was quick to reassure everyone. "As bad as it looks, there isn't pain anymore with it. I can still do everything I used to do and by God's grace, the bullet missed the bone, so no damage there. Many of my buddies are lying cold in the ground for the bullets they took. I'd say without a doubt that I've been truly blessed to have survived at all."

He hitched his pants back together then surveyed each one of us eye-to-eye for a good long moment. "Isn't anything in this world any of you can imagine that is worse than being immersed in all-out war. It's a bloody, angry, constantly changing thing that twists a man's soul in all the wrong directions. Through it all, I just kept telling myself to remember to separate the man I am during my duty to my country from my own daily nature—that is, that man who I am when I'm here.

Those two men are in some ways, very much alike, but now that I am a man at home again, I can feel my true self slowly returning. It was only all of you who kept me going--thinking about getting back home to my family." My brother had never been one to express too much directly from his heart like that. I can still see him standing there proud of having finished his military career and letting all of us know that he was ours again. It was one of the happiest days of my life.

I sat there, as the summary of Denzil's years away continued, unbelieving that this man who once ran around with us in the open grasslands and helped us plant our vegetable crops as a teenaged boy only ten years before, had found himself struggling for his very life halfway around the world. Suddenly, it was all I could do to keep my composure as a grown man myself and I broke down and cried. Upon seeing me crying, my sister Lucy began weeping too and then mother again and then the rest of my sisters. After the wailing ended, Auguste was simply delighted to have his arms wrapped tightly around Denzil. He kept his composure as he talked about the past four years, while the younger brothers sat quietly on the couch with them too. I couldn't seem to get a grip on my emotions that night and I didn't want to seem overly sentimental in front of Father, so I wished everyone a good night and headed up to my room.

The ensuing newspaper accounts of Denzil's heroics in the war, his medals earned and injuries sustained had all been written about even before the town managed to arrange the local hero's parade for him and the few other soldiers who had returned on the same passenger train. Mother and our aunts Lucy and Odette had compiled neatly penned summaries of his actions from his paperwork combined with his first-hand accounts so that Denzil wouldn't need to be bothered by journalists wanting to speak with him. They felt it was too soon after his return. The protective nature of these three women was not going to cease simply because he was a grown man. When they were content with the final copy of these summaries, they carried it into town and delivered it to the newspaper editor themselves. Experience had taught them that newspapers were going to write the story either way, good or bad. It made sense to them that the journalists should get all the facts correct.

After the town threw a ticker-tape parade for the returning soldiers and the mayor gave a speech and bestowed some handmade ribbons upon my brother, life had no other option but to return to normal.

Denzil hadn't been back for even a week when he jumped back into the business of the homestead. He straightaway looked to me then for answers on everything that had changed and adapted quickly to my decisions with regard to the operations. Normally, the whole family would have been working that spring to plant the crops, but there hadn't been enough rain to soften the soil and most of it was dry and compacted hard from the weight of the snow that winter. Now that the entire weight of the farm wasn't squarely on my shoulders, I felt myself growing tired of the long hours and slightly resentful of all that our family had to endure, trying to keep our livelihood going while the lingering effects of war pinched us financially. I needed to know that the extra burden we had all carried had been worth it. I was ready to hear some kind of confirmation from Denzil that his absence really was going to make a difference, locally and in the great big confusing world out there.

I encouraged him to tell his war stories to us whenever possible so that I could understand and make sense of it, but also because I knew that if he carried these memories inside himself without release that they might eat away at his spirit. I had noticed a distinct difference in my brother's demeanor since his return. There were times when he was the same and other times when he seemed to be living in a far distant place, away from all of us. He was quick to question everything and jumpy at unexpected loud noises.

As a young man, Father had never let me forget that I 'wasn't made of the right stuff for military', even though it was entirely his idea to keep me from it. Of course, he was right in his assessment of me, but because of his constant badgering of me during those years, I had become sure that I was cursed to be staying home while Denzil traveled off to foreign lands. In his absence, I had finished my college education. As an aside, I had checked out many books with pictures of European cities from the library. Naively, when I browsed these photos, I envisioned my brother having a time-out now and then from whatever combat his unit was in at the time. I imagined that he probably would be touring quaint villages with shop and restaurants where pretty women served him delicious meals. In some way, I had even, at times, begrudged being an average young man parked by birth on eight hundred acres of farmland in the American heartland. Now, when my older brother did manage to get in the right frame of mind to be able to tell stories about the war; real events of extreme courage and sadness--and even some of cowardice, I finally understood that it was I who had been the lucky one.

The entire family was gathered around the farmhouse fireplace one afternoon in the late summer--our parents, all the brothers and sisters and the aunts on one of their regular visits. I think this afternoon sticks out in my mind because we were celebrating the harvest of a particularly bountiful crop of corn. Not only that, but we had been diversifying our own uses of the corn in ways that we usually ignored. Out of everything we grew, this had become our golden gift from God just when we needed an extra boost. We had new equipment to extract the oil from the corn, we had other equipment that helped us turn it into starch, but mostly we were excited for the added profits off of our family's own corn whiskey. Mother had protested this activity at first, but then when she realized the positive consequences for our family, she conceded. Sure it was illegal, but when the state lawmen in charge of investigating these kinds of businesses were also our customers for it, that hardly mattered anymore.

Denzil had a goal to spin that year's bountiful corn crop into a financial goldmine, including a future plan, in conjunction with other local farmers to produce and sell ethanol, which was very exciting to our family. When he had finished telling war stories and outlining plans for our crops, his captive audience of the three aunts began to say how sorry they were that he had been injured and that he had experienced such human atrocities. Just as he had always done before, Denzil fell back on his mantra: "Nothing to feel sorry about for me," he told them. "It's just the way of the corn."

Inching over closer to where he sat, I nudged him in a way that no one else could see. "Hey," I whispered. "You realize you've been saying that exact thing for at least ten years that I can remember? Never once have you offered to explain this to me—what the hell does it mean? I've grown up since you left, maybe not the same as you but I'm trying to understand the wisdom of the world same as you. Won't you elaborate some—explain how it's so easy for you to just fall back on this as the answer to everything?"

He looked over at my father who was slumped in his chair, smelling of a tell-tale whiskey and fidgeting to get comfortable as he often did before remaining there overnight. "Still sleeping in the chair," Denzil pointed out without answering my question. "What a sight he is, huh? Almost like time is standing still there right before our eyes."

I wanted a real answer from my brother, so I brushed it off. "He hasn't changed because he doesn't see the need. Doesn't want to. So, are you going to answer me or not?"

Denzil took a deep breath and swallowed something distasteful. "Guess it wouldn't make sense to him to change." He walked slowly toward the edge of the room and then nodded his chin upwards for me to follow him. It was a family trait he had picked up from mother and our aunts. Out in the hallway of the great wooden farmhouse, he looked around as if making sure no one else could hear him. Then he said in a low voice, "Go get Lucy and Auguste. I'm going to tell the three of you what you asked me. We'll all take a walk together. I'll explain it."

We sat in the cornfield then that night, like we used to do when we were children—Denzil in the middle sitting upon the red rusted skeleton of the original tractor, my younger sister, Lucy and our middle brother, the skinny tall Auguste who loomed over me like a scarecrow figure, standing there under a full moon watching nightbirds flying high overhead through glowing clouds, while the bats swooped in the space of sky nearest us. Now and then some kind of night creature traveling on the ground would rub itself against the corn stalks and we could trace down the rows where it went and imagine how big it probably was by observing the tops of the golden silks waving, a few seconds at a time. While I kept a nervous watch over the movement in the corn rows--because I still believed that there were panthers or lions in Kansas-- Auguste, Lucy and I sat still and attentive, waiting.

There was a bit of weariness in his eyes and Denzil began speaking slowly as if rushing the words would cause us to miss the essence of his beliefs. "So Marc keeps asking me about this thing that I've always said to explain away the happenings in life, so that it all makes sense. I asked you, Lucy and Auguste, to come out here too while I explain it to him because you are probably the only siblings I have who will actually listen to what I mean to say."

For a moment, he struggled to speak as if some memory had crept into his heart and was fighting for his attention. Then I saw a resolve come over his face to focus on what he needed to tell us. "Corn has a way about it, just like the souls and destinies of men," he said. "It lives. It lives within the shell of a seed knowing who and what it is even before we can see that it is anything. A simple yellow seed. There's an intelligence put into it by God just as he has put that same intelligence into us to know who we are. So corn; it either struggles to survive against all adverse conditions or it thrives wholeheartedly under the blessings of sunlight and rain. By its nature, corn plunges its roots firmly into the soil, whether it be sandy or hard like clay and it knows--it knows, by God--that no matter what comes, it will stand its ground. Even when conditions aren't what they should be, there's a good chance that corn is going to survive. It survives only due to its inner knowing, just like we do. And it has a purpose...many purposes

145

sometimes. Either way, we and corn also eventually die. Corn, like us, has its own predestined seasons of birth and rebirth."

"Birth and rebirth?" I repeated as a question. "What the hell is that kind of talk Denzil? You forgetting we're Lutherans and don't believe in that sort of shit?"

"Don't 'shit' up what I just said, Marc," he snapped at me. "I thought you really wanted to know. You're the one who asked me to explain, remember? Be humble now and then. Listen seriously to exactly what I just said. Let it sink into your mind and swim around a bit--sink into your heart--and maybe then you can then accept all the madness that our lives have had to endure so far. This has been my mantra when I speak about the way of the corn. What I've told you has kept me standing tall in every situation since I first understood it. I spent hours and days out here in this very cornfield as a young teenager before it came to me. Funny thing is, for all the church services we attended I never heard the voice of God there. I don't know; maybe it was all the singing and the preaching and the focus on all of us dressed in our Sunday best. It was here where I connected to God. Right out here in a cornfield, in the middle of nowhere. I used to come out here and talk to God. I have no doubt at all that in the silence of this place, he guided me and helped me make some very important decisions. Nobody told me any of this. It's something I suddenly knew without a doubt. If each of you weren't so quick to answer everything with the first ideas that pop into your head, you might take in what I'm saying with some weight upon your own lives."

"What the hell kind of talk is that?" I asked. "You talk in circles, like life is some great mystery." I was agitated with the way he still took liberties in speaking to us as if we were mere children, under his wing in some way. Even so, I had respect for him. "I get it now," I said because I wanted desperately to try to grasp what he had told us. "I'll think about it more seriously and maybe it'll help me to make decisions, too."

"Yeah, it makes sense," Auguste said. "We're each like this one insignificant grain of corn with something imprinted on us from the beginning by our creator to know who we are and to survive whatever comes. You're kinda' saying that the way of the corn is actually God's plan for us and to accept our challenges and our successes as if it is part of a greater plan."

Denzil pointed at Auguste and clapped as one does for a great statesman who has just made a memorable speech. "Yes! Yes! You get it now," he said. "I think all of you get it now."

"It's so poetic," Lucy chimed in. "I never knew you to be so deep, my dear brother Denzil." She gave him one of her trademark bear hugs without letting go, and I could tell it made him feel awkward but he let her do it all the same.

We sat there that night, the four of us, grown up adults, yet still mystified by the moonlight and the beauty of an open sky for another hour or so, just enjoying that we were once again, all together. I don't remember ever feeling closer to those three siblings than I did on that night.

CHAPTER EIGHT

Our father had got wind of some information about a POW camp in Kansas where nearly four thousand German prisoners had been held. Many of this group had been captured in the North African battles and under the rules of the Geneva Convention, had been housed in fairly decent quarters, awaiting the end of the war. Most of these men were returned home to Germany after the war ended. However; there were several who remained behind. These men had petitioned for permission to immigrate to the United States permanently.

Apparently, several of these former captives who chose to stay behind and restart their lives in America had already found work as skilled stonemasons or as laborers on other farms. In a weird twist, my father had appointed Denzil and I to go to this German prisoner camp and inquire if one of them wanted to hire on as an extra worker at our farm. I had my doubts that Denzil was the right person to ask considering that these men were viewed as his enemy very recently. Whether out of a natural curiosity or some other more personal reason, my eldest brother agreed without hesitation.

We had taken the family car, Denzil and I again, like old times. I could see that he was preoccupied, probably rehearsing what he was going to say when we arrived at our destination. He was in the habit of being prepared, but I noticed after his stint in the war, his preparation of every day had become much more intense.

I interrupted his silent thoughts. "How will we know if we can trust these former soldiers of the enemy or not once we get there, assuming any of them will agree to work for us? Doesn't sound safe, in fact to me, it's a downright dangerous idea," I advised.

Denzil wasn't deterred by my concerns. He had been sent on a mission by our father and our goal was to carry it out with success. "We won't ever know unless we look into it. I'm guessing if a man stays behind in another country after being held as a prisoner of war for a couple years that there's something he dislikes about his own country or that he has discovered something about our way of life he likes. And I, personally, want to know exactly why they'd like to stay here in America."

"So a few months back they were our sworn enemies and now they're our damn friends?" I asked, giving him a dose of the same kind of logic he was always only too eager to use on me.

"I don't have the answer to that and I suppose, me of all people, I should. This is part of why we're going there-- to find out. We're also going to find out something about ourselves, I think, by being willing to consider this new idea. I can only hope it won't bring a slew of negative sentiment upon our household. Our country has sacrificed its soul for the war effort and it's going to be tricky to get anyone, me included, to accept this kind of foreigner into our lives. The Mexican workers are one type of people, but these, I can tell you from firsthand experience, are quite another."

All at once, it became clear to me. This new idea wasn't only about finding help for our farm. My brother was also trying to work out his personal feelings about the war. "Well, I've gotta say I'm fairly against this but of course, since you're back and since father wants us to do it; I'm along to concede to your decision," I said. This was one time when I was relieved to be sitting in the background of a decision. After running the bulk of the homestead operations for so long, even with a remarkably successful outcome, I was relieved to let Denzil take the lead again.

When we arrived for our appointment at Camp Concordia as it was called, we were introduced to a man around the age of forty named Werner who apparently had grown up in a farming community in his homeland. To me, he didn't look much different than any other

European immigrants we knew locally, except for his marked friendliness and that his accent was different. He appeared well-fed and wore nice clothes, same as ours. After a lengthy three-hour interview with Denzil, wherein I remained silent and only listened, he claimed to be skilled with horses and cattle as well as being a fairly good mechanic. He had no problem when Denzil insisted that he would be sworn to uphold the laws and traditions of our country, including signing his name to this as quickly as it could be written down on paper. After that, they finally agreed by a handshake to some kind of monetary terms.

Then, as we all stood to leave the room where the interview was held, Denzil issued the former natural German citizen a stern caveat. "And we will not be discussing the war. We can talk about many things together when you are settled at the farm, but never about that."

Werner closed his eyes and made a sad face for a few seconds, then nodded that he understood. We walked down a hallway with him to a room that was furnished with a cot and an old wooden armoire. There, he gathered his belongings, handing me an extra cardboard box to carry for him when his arms became overloaded. Then, at a custodian office he was given his paperwork and another box of belongings by the camp authorities. Another hour later, after a rather quiet meal at a roadside stop; we were driving back towards the family homestead with a new German farmhand who spoke fairly good English.

On the way, my brother started up the conversation again by relaying that he had been in France and Germany during the war, fighting for the US Army. I had purposely seated myself in the backseat, letting Werner sit beside Denzil, as a backup position in case anything went wrong.

"I thought we weren't going to talk about the war?" Werner reminded him as a question.

"We're not going to talk about the details of the war," Denzil said. "But I want you to know that I was there. I did my part in the war for my country."

"I see," Werner answered. "So you volunteered? Or did they knock up your door and say 'you are obligated to come with us?'"

"Well, it didn't work quite like that, but I was drafted. By means of a letter. We all had to register with selective service at a certain age, but I was notified of my draft by a letter received in the mail," Denzil clarified. "Still, I'd have volunteered to fight in the war if I knew I was needed. Truthfully, I was still just a young man from a farm in Kansas who didn't know much about the world out there, only about the people living in our own county and a few counties surrounding ours. My view of the world was based on what I read in books during school and of course, through stories our family told about their lives in France before immigrating here."

"Same," said Werner, gazing out the window onto the flat fields of corn stretching out to the horizon. "I had no idea what America looked like, how vast it really is. How the people are. I still don't as I haven't actually been travelling you know." They both laughed. "I don't need to go back to the country I was born into," Werner continued. "This will be my country now. A new land. A new family. My family is mostly gone and I never got married to have children."

"Were they killed in the war—your family that is?" Denzil had to ask and I shuddered as he said it. It just seemed too soon to ask such a question and we were veering into the territory that had been agreed upon to avoid.

"Not the war. My parents were older when they had me. I was the only child they got. It was a shame because they loved children so much. Any event...they died before the war which I am somewhat glad of because they would not have approved of it at all. They certainly would not have approved of them taking me into service to do their bidding. So that was the only family I had besides one very old uncle. Of course, I was in love with a girl once some years before that, but since I didn't admit how much I loved her I lost her to another man. My ego mattered to me at that time much more than the willpower to try. So, yeah--she met this other man who was willing to put his proud self on the line and declare his love for her and that is the one to whom she is married."

"That's sad," I said. "My brother used to love this girl from Kansas City...."

"Don't get into that," Denzil interrupted, looking at me through the rearview mirror.

"Oh yes, please get into it," Werner coaxed me. He positioned himself so that he could see me better in the backseat. He smiled with anticipation. "I'd really like to hear this story." He shot an almost teasing look over at my brother. "Continue, Brother Marc. Tell about this woman now. I haven't heard anything but gloomy bloody war reports for two years now. It will be fine to hear a love story for once."

So I continued, even with the risk of making my brother mad. "Well, it's quite simple that this woman from Kansas City was really making my brother happy," I said. "So happy in fact, that I was actually getting a little jealous because he spent more time with her than with me. We had always been inseparable, you know?"

"I see. Like the first real girlfriend for your brother."

"Not really," I said, talking about my brother as if he weren't in the car with us, but noticing by his expression, his interest in hearing my version of the events. "Actually, my brother had many, many real girlfriends before this woman."

"They couldn't have all been real like that," Werner said. "That's not how it works at all. And I should know I had plenty of girlfriends before the real one too," he nudged Denzil with his elbow, in comradery. "Oh yes, I knew the difference. So what was the name of this kind of best girlfriend when you noticed your brother spending so much time with her?"

"Bernadette," said Denzil in a way that I hadn't heard him say her name in so many years. He spoke her name with each letter of it carefully escaping him like something cherished still.

I continued. "Yes, Bernadette was my brother's best kind of girlfriend I had ever seen him with, but there was one small problem." I paused and looked cautiously at my brother not sure if I should really tell the rest of his private story in the way that I was telling it. I tried to think of a way to say the truth without making Denzil angry or defensive.

Werner fidgeted around in the front seat as I leaned over closer from the backseat between he and my brother. Clearly, he was practically going giddy waiting to know what happened. In the long drive between the camp that had been his dubious home and onwards to our farmland many more miles down the road, he had endeared himself to us so that he now was involved with my brother's love story. "And the problem was?"

"Ophelia," I stated flatly.

"What in the hell is that—Ophelia?" he repeated.

"It's a woman's name," I said.

Werner laughed out loud and rattled his own face back and forth in his hands, as if to straighten his thoughts out. "It sounds like 'I feel you!" he shouted.

"That's what I always said," I confessed, smiling.

"She was another woman that I liked," Denzil answered as if he were getting annoyed at me and as if Werner were an idiot. "Another woman that Bernadette found out about and she never forgave me. So I lost her. Should've tried to get her back, and I guess I did try for a while. Then I just gave up."

"Aha! Now this is so clear!" Werner exclaimed, gesturing to the sky with his hands. "I can see this now. Well, that is where you French-American half breeds don't have a thing over us Germans if I can be so bold as to tell you."

"Whoah, whoah, whoah!" Denzil said, raising his voice. "Is that what they, the Germans, tell you to call us--half breeds? No. In America we might be people sometimes with a couple of different backgrounds; and just so you know our family was one-hundred-percent French heritage, but we don't say 'half breeds'. We just are Americans. Or sometimes we are Italian-Americans or German-Americans, see? So be careful what you say with that. Maybe it is what you were taught to be as bold as possible and just say whatever first thing comes to mind, but you must think more before you speak in this country."

"I have offended you already," Werner said, clearly not remorseful but rather amused. "I'm sorry, lover boy, but I was only trying to get to the crux of the matter as they say. Just that my error of words has annoyed you tells me that you still must have some emotions for this Bernadette woman. The conversation has hit a nerve in yourself. What I was about to point out is that, well okay; maybe the French have always had a reputation for not fighting too hard for something they want, whereas the German man, he will pursue a woman he loves with everything he's got before he gives her up if it is his real love. Except for me: I did not." He sat back in his seat proud of his contribution to the story and clasped his hands together. "So that's it. You made a choice to give up easily, same as I did when I should have been the bolder man and not worried about my ego so much. But maybe for me it wasn't a real love; maybe it only seemed that way at the time. For you, in your case, I think even if you had made such a terrible mistake of your heart, there was probably a way to fix it."

"Well, no point talking about it now," Denzil said. "Probably same as your girlfriend, she's surely married to another by now."

After a couple hours more of a quiet car ride, where Denzil drove and Werner and I slept in our seats, Denzil barked a command for us to wake up. As we slowly came back to life, my brother seemed relieved to open up the talks again, this time about another subject. The first open field of our family's eight hundred acres had come into view. "This is your new home Werner," Denzil said, gesturing with a wide swath of his hand and pointing at the farmhouse--a mere speck in the distance.

"It's wonderful!" Werner breathed as if he were literally soaking it all into his being. The vast rows of apple orchards were in bloom and with the windows down, the faint smell of their flowers hung on the air. As the farmhouse came closer into view, tears began to form in his eyes. "I'm sorry about the crying but this is like my big event. A big event in my heart."

I tapped his shoulder a couple times. "I understand," I said. "Now the fun part begins."

Denzil parked the car near the front entrance of the farmhouse and we all stepped out of the car into the hot afternoon Kansas sun. After making a 360 degree circle with his arms outstretched, as if to pull it all in at once, and after surveying the farmhouse itself from bottom-to-top, Werner spontaneously grabbed my brother and me around our necks, pulling us in on each side of him in a sort of a rough, jostling hug of comradery. "Oh, what a fine house, all made of wood and the tin roof! And this fresh air. I can't find words to tell you how I have actually dreamed of having a home like this in America," Werner said. "Even if I'm your employee I shall treat your home, this place, with the respect as if it were my own. You will see; I shall treat your family as if you were my own too."

As we unloaded the pillows and boxes from the car, Denzil looked at me, then back at Werner who was already, suitcase in-hand, headed up to the front door by himself. "Dear God in heaven; what have we done now, Marc?" Denzil whispered to me. "We'd better get inside and make the introductions and show him to his living quarters."

It didn't take long for Werner to make a friend of each family member on that first night. They all stayed up to hear him talk about growing up in Germany before Father finally called an end to the fun by reminding Werner that he was there to work and that sunrise came very early on a farm.

* * *

I wondered if I would ever meet someone or love someone, as I knew my brother had once loved the girl from Kansas City. I had been inspired by the story that Werner shared with us about losing the love of his life. It didn't seem fair to me that after finding the one you know you're supposed to be with, that it could possibly fall apart by misunderstandings or careless behavior. My brother had been careless with love in his younger years, but it didn't lessen the fact that he was still carrying around her memory, like a perfectly prepared house with an open door waiting for a visitor who never arrives.

It was after dark already when I began to rustle around, upstairs in my room, quietly as I could so I wouldn't wake the rest of the household. After pulling back the curtains to see that the moon was right—just enough bright beams streaming through the window and lighting up the wall to let me know it was a good night for traveling—I grabbed a suitcase out of the closet and stuffed a change of clothes into it. Then I tiptoed down the stairs, looking up behind me for movement as the creaking threatened to give me away. When I was sure that no one was watching, I headed out to my car. I sat inside the car long enough to pen a note and stick it on the nail next to the front door where people left notes, so that Mother wouldn't get worried when I didn't return for dinner the next evening. I drove many hours through the long night towards Kansas City where I rented a motel room.

The next morning, I started my search for Bernadette at the last place I could recall hearing about—the school where future secretaries were hatched. After convincing the records-keeper there that my inquiry was romantic and not malicious, I learned that my brother's long lost love was now working at the office of the governor in Topeka. An address was offered and I took it gratefully. On the long drive back home, I imagined how thrilled Denzil would be to ever receive a letter from her. I knew that it would be up to me to take the first steps, even if I had to admit that there was also a sliver of fear for what he might do if my assumptions about his feelings were somehow wrong. I was also assuming that she had not married which could have been uncomfortable for me to find out.

That same evening, using my brother's name (not mine) I penned a long apologetic letter for my past behavior, admitted that I had been a complete jackass and a young fool and stated my undying love for Bernadette. The next morning I drove into town with the letter, had it stamped at the post office and dropped it into the general mail bin. I could have put it in our rural delivery box, but I wasn't taking any chances of it falling into someone else's curious hands.

In the long days that followed, I monitored our family's mailbox religiously so that no one in the house might intercept the letter that I anticipated would follow. It seemed like more than a week went by before there it was lying there in the box—a reply from Bernadette. I quickly slurked it into the house and steamed the envelope open, fighting my conscience all the while wondering if it was considered reading another's mail when it was really me who had initiated the contact. Upstairs in my room, I read some very personal words addressed to my brother, typed neatly and folded just so. The most important thing she said in it was that she 'was still longing for him too and if he wanted to drive to the capital sometime, it would be the best day she had known for all these years'. She penned her name and a telephone number at the bottom.

Now, it would be do-or-die time for Denzil. First, I needed to be sure that I wasn't into this plot over my head. I still had not held any kind of relationship of my own for longer than six months, so my anxiety with the thing was growing by the minute. My Aunt Odette had always been a great confidante of mine and seemed to know quite a bit more than me about other people's feelings. It was time to get a female's view of the situation. I decided to drive to her house in town and spill out my plan to her for approval.

When I told her about the progress I had made so far, let her read the letter from Bernadette and asked for her advice, Aunt Odette just smiled, seeming to know that I would do whatever I wanted anyway. "Either way," she advised me, "he's probably often thinking about her whereabouts and maybe he does want to know whatever became of her. If he chooses not to see her, after she has written back this letter that would seem foolish on his part. I think he did love her as much as you say too." Aunt Odette then cautioned me about meddling too insistently in other people's lives. "Even though you mean well, there could have been unseen reasons keeping them apart too. Sometimes things really are better left buried."

"You mean better left in the past? Even love?"

"Yes. Even love. If it didn't work out between them, there's obviously a reason. There's no way to know how he's going to react though. I'd say knowing Denzil as we do though, that you might get told a thing or two about meddling in his personal affairs. So be prepared for that."

I left my aunt's house more confused than before I arrived, especially knowing that she had meddled in the romantic affairs of many people and usually with positive results. On the way back home, I resolved in my heart and mind that I had not tracked down Bernadette for nothing. There were good intentions steering my actions and if I were going to be admonished by my brother for that; then it would be worth the risk. He was going to read her letter. There was no turning back for me.

As the sun went down, I skipped past the kitchen before anyone could see me with the letter in-hand. I knew if one of my sisters saw me walking around the house with a letter in my hand, they would start asking questions and it didn't feel right to shove it in my pocket for some reason, as it wasn't really mine. My nervousness about the entire plan was causing me to behave abnormally. Taking one of the older farm trucks, I drove down an access road toward a dim glowing light in the distance. I found Denzil working in the main tool shed, cleaning up after the bracero bunch had finished for the night. He never felt entirely comfortable with the way they left things and had developed the habit of inspecting their work.

"Answer me something honest," I said, as I always had before when seeking advice for myself.

"Sure," he said.

"You really, really were in love with that young lady named Bernadette, weren't you, Denzil?" I asked straight out.

He had grown used to my odd questions by then. He had learned to just answer me or there would only be more to follow. "To be honest with you--yeah. I really, really was. It was certainly an entertaining story that you told Werner. At least he enjoyed hearing about it." He shook his head at the memory and snickered to himself. "Let that be a lesson to you from your older brother then. Two women and one stupid man never makes for a love story. If you want to find love yourself, don't do what I did. Instead of trying to find the right woman like a fox picking up a chicken in its mouth, then seeing a better chicken, dropping it for the next, and the next and so on...well, you just realize that the one you had first might have been everything you needed."

"You've always had the strangest way to explain things. I'm talking women and you're talking foxes and chickens."

"Okay, Marc. Then; just work on you being the right man. That right woman will come along for you someday."

"I'm not talking about me," I said. I handed him the letter. "I'm talking about you."

He took it, then opened it quickly as if fearing bad news. I watched him read it before folding it carefully again. "You did this? You did this for me? Why would you do such a thing? How'd you do this?"

The expression on his face told me that I had done the right thing. I was instantly relieved. "I told you before; I'm smarter than you've ever given me credit for. Now and then I get it right. I did get it right didn't I, Denzil?" I asked, relishing the thought of hearing the words.

"Damn right; you got it right!" he shouted out. He wrapped his arms around me and jumped me up and down in place with him a couple times, nearly crushing my ribs. "I can't believe this!" he shouted out to the sky. "What am I gonna' do now?" I watched him pace the ground in a bunch of crazed angles and half-circles as if his mind was creating a roadmap to Topeka.

Watching my brother completely lose control of his well-trained demeanor was thoroughly delightful. He had always been the strong one, the willfully composed one. I had unraveled him, in the best way, with this piece of news. I felt like I had given him the greatest gift he had ever received.

Denzil took the train to Topeka the following day. Three days later, when he returned, Bernadette was with him and they had done more than just catch up on old times. They had decided to never let anything come between them again. Not another woman or man. Not war. Not anything. A judge had performed their marriage ceremony right in the state capital building. Denzil had packed all of her belongings from her rented room into the car and headed back home to the farm where he had promised to build them a house somewhere on the property. After the whole family got over the shock of their unexpected news, the women invited everyone we knew to come out to the farm for that weekend. It was a tremendous feast to celebrate my brother and his new wife. I couldn't have been more pleased to be the cause of all the happiness.

* * *

The Spanish braceros who lived on the farm with us now, had graciously begun to refer to our home as their home. In the same way, Werner had settled in to a work routine that suited him and had already begun to help our operations tremendously. Denzil had said more than once that it had been mostly the thought of each person back on the farm that had helped him stay strong during the war and fight unthinkable battles. He had often told us of repeating the braceros' sentiments of home to himself as a reminder that he needed to somehow survive and get back to the country he loved and the place where he was born. There was a reason why his life had been spared—now he would go forward into the next chapter of life as a husband. The addition of Bernadette to our family would only plunge our roots deeper into the land. My oldest brother's odd corn mantra was starting to make sense to me as well, and I had no doubt that it would continue carrying him through whatever life had in store for him.

After Denzil settled into married life for a few months, we all noticed a change in him. He was beginning to build the home he had promised Bernadette, on the ten acres abutting the barn that had never been used for farming. Besides his focus on that, he was noticeably even more introspective about things than ever before. I approached him as he sat on the tractor seat early one morning, twirling one of those grass seed stems that we used to pull up and pull apart when we were kids. Lucy used to talk certain kids into holding one loosely in their teeth--'for just a moment while I show you a trick'--she'd say. Then after they were transfixed on her mischievous eyes, waiting to see something magical, she'd give a quick left-side pull to the solid stem leaving the kid with a mouth full of fuzzy seeds.

Perhaps he's remembering those days, I thought. "You alright?" I asked, aware that he wasn't his usual smiling self, but rather looked outward over the field as if he were actually far away. I climbed up on the tractor, leaning against the engine cover, holding onto the stack for balance.

He didn't look away from the field, as if taking his eyes off of it would cause him to lose his train of thought. "There're things in this life that I wish I could share with you."

"Ah, the war memories again, is it?" I asked.

"No...things you don't know, or couldn't possibly remember," Denzil said to me. "I've wrestled my urges to take a look backwards and always, the answer came to me to let things be. Then I think, 'am I letting things be for my own protection or because it's right?' So many times, when I drive the flatbed produce truck into town, down that long bumpy dirt road, I've taken the time to review my life—review things I've been through--and wonder 'what's the point of it all?' It occurred to me one day, looking in my rear-view mirror, that all that jumbled-up world behind us just gets smaller and smaller the further away you travel. That mirror seems purposely made small like that; it's like a compressed image that holds the past. But then, the windshield— well, it's wide and open, to see everything. It's like your whole future just spread out there waiting. And--It's been designed to be much wider and taller than the mirrors on each side that also point to the past. So you're driving along and you have this big windshield urging you to go forward with a clear view. All these possibilities you can't even see out there, waiting around the corner. It's truly one of the most profound realizations I've ever had in my life and just cements what I've always believed about the way of the corn."

It was in moments such as this that I had developed true admiration for my brother. There weren't very many people in our simple rural community who I knew, talking about life in such a way as that. Decisions in life locally had been, over the years, decided through the interpretations of biblical text, the educated discernment of the local judges and the cumulative opinion of a bevy of women who made it their business to sort out anyone who wasn't living in the right way.

Denzil had always possessed an introspective nature that you just didn't see in the rural countryside. People where we lived were mostly focused on whatever it took to survive from one season to the next. They didn't take the time to ponder corn and mirrors and futures outside of a windshield too much.

I put my arm around Denzil's shoulders supportively. "You're home now, my brother. And that future's going to be more than either of us could have imagined when we were just little grasshoppers running around wild out here. I mean, look at me—college graduate now and everything. And you--married. Who would've believed that back when?

He leaned his head into my shoulder. I instinctively wrapped my arms around him. Without looking up from the grassy plume he was holding he said, "Still Marc, some of those things back there in the rearview mirror constantly nag at me, asking me to bring them to light. I resist going back there because I don't wanna' unearth pain. You understand me don't you?" He pulled away and looked straight into my eyes.

I thought about if the question were reversed. How would he counsel me? "Get it off your conscience," I prodded. "It's eating away at you or you wouldn't bring it up to me, the closest person you've got of all the brothers and sisters or our parents. Surely you know by now that your concerns, whatever they are—they're going to be the same as mine, even if I don't know about them yet. That's just how brothers like us are. Whatever are you talking about?"

"Can you keep something quiet? I mean more quiet than the most secretive trouble you and I ever got into together?" There was an uneasy quivering in his voice that I had never heard before. He hesitated for a moment and I thought he was reconsidering what he needed to say.

"Beyond Double-Top-Secret?" I said, reverting back humorously to our childhood code.

"Right. That you will spend your whole life carrying and not speaking about."

"You know, if you ask me...you're my oldest brother. More than that; you've always been my best friend. I'm not gonna' tell a soul if that's how you say it should be, Denzil. I promise I won't tell. Tell me."

He inhaled quickly and blew out the same way. He had obviously thought about this moment for a very long while before considering letting it out. "A long time ago, when you were about four years old and I was about ten, our mother had another husband who died. This was before Marne and Auguste were born. Before Charles and Cain."

The words hit me like a hard smack in the head. "What?!" I shouted out, jumping up immediately and saying the first thing that came to my mind. "Hell, Denzil; that would mean that you and I and the others aren't the same siblings as we thought we were."

"Shut up!" My brother said abruptly. "I knew you were going to say that, but it's not that way. We've grown up together and are all just as much brothers and sisters to each other as any other. If our parents found you or Samuel or Auguste or Marne, any of us, under a damn rock, you all wouldn't be any less my siblings! If you're going to react like a lunatic even before I tell you the worst part, I'm not going to tell you anything at all."

"I'm doing it again, aren't I?" I said honestly humble but confused. "Okay. You're right. I said I'd listen and now I will. I'll manage whatever it is you want to tell me."

"Yeah; you are doing it again. And I'm also going to swear you to secrecy that you'll never discuss these things with our mother either."

He was on the edge of getting angry at me. I settled myself inside and asked, "Because it would upset her?"

"Of course, it would be more than upsetting. This is something that our father surely doesn't even know every piece of. But I don't want her to know that I told you. It would be like opening up a deep sewed-up wound upon her very flesh. I know you love her deeply as I do and I won't have it under any circumstances. You understand?"

My simple mind was reeling, but I wanted to let my brother know that somewhere within me I had the capacity to be a solid dependable guy. I wanted him to know that I was loyal to his wishes. "I told you whatever you say is between us. I promised and I meant it, Denzil. I'm good for my word and you know it. Please tell me."

"Well, as I started to say, mother had another husband. As I grew up, I watched her struggle and fall victim to this man in ways that can make even a child angry inside. And this anger built up in me from the times of my

179

earliest memories. I watched her wait for him for what seemed like weeks at a time to return from somewhere, only to slap her and me too whenever his temper started raging. He'd slap her across the face, shove her down to the floor, grit his teeth and rage into her face saying all kinds of horrible things.

When he would leave on another trip, usually loaded up with our crops, it was almost a relief--as mother would settle down and we'd have this glorious space of time, sometimes a couple days, sometimes a week at least. We'd tend to the animal chores and work the crops together. Sometimes we'd sit at the big wooden table and she'd draw animal pictures for me to color in with crayons. The farm was much smaller then and even at my young age, I was a big help to our mother, I know. In the evenings, after she put you and Lucy down to sleep for the night, she'd come back downstairs and we'd sing songs together or play dance tunes on the old phonograph. Many nights we could hear the locust outside singing like a hundred backup singers to the music. Her sisters didn't visit as much as they do now. I don't know why. Maybe they didn't like mother's first husband and this made them stay away, but I remember really wishing they would come around more as it made me feel safer. Anyway, sometimes when it was only us on this big property all by ourselves, she'd sit in the rocking chair and take her hair down out of the pins. Her hair would almost touch the floor, it was so long then. She'd hand me her hairbrush and ask me to help her with smoothing it out. It was like I was more than just her son; I was her closest friend too. But I must admit that the quiet was unnerving when coyotes would start yowling in the distance. I always feared one of them would come and drag me off the front porch or something. So I gained a sort of sixth sense about everything going on around me."

"You're right. I haven't the slightest memory of this or anything before maybe five years old now that I think about it. So anyway, if things were this bad, you probably didn't give a care when our first father returned home, then? What did you and mother need him for if all he did was make it hard for her to care for all of us? Well, did he finally leave for good then?"

"Just a minute. I'm getting to it. The thing is, we wouldn't have much food—not just a shortage of food; I mean he didn't leave us with any means to get by. Whenever he left, he'd take the whole crops and 'go carousing into town' as mother said, and sell everything. I'd always ask her when we were going to see the money from the crops as I knew that him bringing home the money meant that we would be able to keep the house going, to have food besides only what we were growing—to be able to survive. She'd always tell me not to ever ask that in front of him and to just wait that things would get better. As this continued, I watched how mother kept going, admiring the way she was able to keep us fed. The little things she did to set aside provisions for us. Like I would see her fishing through his pants pockets in the middle of the night after he got back, collecting some coins which she hid in a large flower vase in my bedroom. Always with a wink, she'd put a finger to her lips as if to say it was a secret for only she and I.

He'd never stay for long before leaving again. It was like watching a miracle seeing how many ways she could cut a single ham sandwich to feed lunch to the three of us. And I can still hear in the dead of night out in these very fields how she used to sing to me after we would trudge out here, if the weather was nice and the coyotes weren't being seen around, to sit on this old rusted tractor."

Denzil knocked the metal on the tractor a couple of times with his knuckles. "Yeah, she used to look much better back then."

"Who?" I asked. "The tractor or Mother?"

"The tractor is what I mean, you goofball. Don't you ever read between the lines?"

"I'm going to be a writer someday Denzil," I blurted out. "I'm actually going to be reading *and* writing between the lines. So go on now and tell me, so this first father of ours was a real son-of-a-bitch, not taking care of our family properly. Did he run off then for good, eventually?"

"Not exactly," Denzil said with that kind of twisted-up grin that scared me sometimes. "And this isn't anything you're ever going to write about, so forget it. I don't even know why you would say that because that isn't what we're talking about. Yeah, so as I was saying...things got worse before they got better. Sometimes a visitor from town would come out and sit with me and you because you were a baby then. Or they'd stay overnight in the parlor while mother and us slept upstairs so we wouldn't have to be alone anymore. I thought that was the nicest thing in the world. I wondered if I would ever do anything as noble when I grew into a man--to travel for miles to someone's house in the middle of nowhere, just to keep some other people from being alone.

Anyway, one of those people in later years was the man we now know as our father. But I'm getting too far ahead. You want to know what happened to our first father, first."

I suddenly felt like I had an ant's nest churning inside my head. "Right, Denzil." I felt myself getting annoyed. "Why can't you just tell a thing straight out? Why all the background stories and years and years leading up to stuff? We're both grown men. You can just blurt out the whole thing in about five sentences can't you?"

He jumped down off the tractor and paced around in a circle as he talked, like a wristwatch wound up too tight then releasing a spring before ticking again. "I'm not about to tell something like what I have to tell you in a careless or slight way. It wouldn't be telling all the truth. Without knowing all of the truth about things, you can't make up your own mind one way or another whether or not to understand it properly."

"What the hell are you talking about?" I yelled out. "You're starting to make no sense. I felt an anger boiling up from nowhere at all. You know something about our life, something that affects both of us now and you're only letting out bits at a time."

"Truth is, my brother, is that nothing of what I'm about to tell you affects the life either of us know now--at all! We have lived good healthy, fairly normal lives despite a background of horrible happenings which before today, never even entered into your reality. But this has been a part of my reality, the reality in my heart, for many years. Now that I'm married and possibly going to be a father myself someday down the line, I'm beginning to look back upon my life—wondering how I got to be the way I am."

"Sorry," I said. "You're right. Isn't anything that can change the bond between us anyway and that's a promise. You believe me don't you?"

"I've known that my whole life, brother. Nothing about that's going to change unless it changed on your part."

"Go on then," I said.

"So on one night, this first husband, who I would never even dream to call my father or yours; he comes home from town angry and yelling. Mother and I had been upstairs, propped up with pillows on her bed, reading a book together. I remember you were sleeping in your crib. When he came in, she seemed to know he was in a really bad way and so she sent me to my room down the hall. Before she could get even halfway down the stairs, he flies up there ranting and raving about how the house wasn't clean and because the front door had been left propped open that a bat had flown into the house. I looked out my bedroom door and saw him grabbing her by her hair. Then he shoved our mother down the stairs! She laid completely still at the bottom and when I rushed to the top looking down, it did seem to me like she was actually dead! I was scared out of my mind at the thought. But then I heard her moaning. He looked up the stairwell at me and yelled out, 'Don't stand there staring like an idiot. Go to your room'."

Denzil put both hands, fingers curled up covering his eyes, remembering. He continued. "To which I shouted in the strongest voice I'd ever heard come out of my own body, 'No!'. He marched up the stairs leaving Mother still lying at the bottom of the stairs. I remember feeling

186

happy in that moment, because I had caused him to leave her alone, but I realized in an instant that he was probably going to beat on me now. So I high-tailed it for my room, closing the door behind me, turning the key quickly. In an instant, I could hear him breathing angrily on the other side. Then his footsteps began treading back down the hallway, fading away and then going back down the stairs. For a moment, I felt safe. Then I felt like a worthless coward, if a kid even knows what that is. I just couldn't stay locked safely in my room, knowing that our mother was probably being kicked on the floor or choked or God knows what. I made the decision to unlock the door."

"Were you scared?"

"Jesus! Was I scared? I knew in my heart what I had to do yet my legs wouldn't stop shaking barely enough to hold up my own weight. I was so scared that as I approached the stairwell again I could feel the warm pee going down my leg. Somehow, I was able to shake off the embarrassment of that, telling myself that it didn't matter as much as what I was going to do. At that point, I had it locked in my mind, just as one locks his ammunition into a gun with the intention to fire upon an enemy. At that point in time, the thing that was going to happen was a direct line in my mind from where I stood up to the point where that man would not be breathing with life ever again."

"Could mother see you coming down the stairs? Did she say anything to you?"

"He had dragged her into the kitchen area and was telling her to stand up and was kicking her in the ribs as she laid on the floor. I could hear him tell her to get up and go tend to me in my room because she had caused me to be scared. She pleaded with him--said that she was hurt and couldn't make it up the stairs. He continued screaming at her that she was 'a poor excuse for a mother', 'letting a bat get into a house where children lay sleeping', things like that. I nearly broke into tears to hear that because to me, she had been perfect." Denzil put knuckles to his teeth and bit lightly. His head was down and he was rubbing his foot around in the dry dirt and rocks. I could tell he was fighting back tears, so I stayed silent until he could gather himself again.

"The best mother ever," he said, finally breaking down and crying. "I loved her more than anybody and I knew that him saying that to her had to be breaking her heart. I didn't dare cry though because I feared so much what might happen if he heard me. So I came around the side of the wall staying at a place where the shadow covered me, not letting the dim kitchen light give me away. While he was kneeling over her, hitting her in the ribs some more and screaming like someone from a madhouse, I picked up the black iron poker from the pot-bellied stove and with every muscle in me, I crashed it down upon the back of his skull. I had hit him with such a force that the iron rang out when it made contact with bone. The vibration of it ran up to my arm and disappeared along with his life. The body dropped to the floor like a canvas sack of grain and didn't even move a twitch. He never even got the chance to turn around and see that it was me who had done him in." Denzil stopped talking, wiped the tears away from his cheeks with resolve and took a deep breath, gazing again far off into the distance.

I sensed his relief in having told me this secret after all these years. My head suddenly felt like it was full of water. Emotions were welling up within me as I tried to take it all in within the brief period of a few seconds without the dam inside my head just giving way. I wanted to cry like I had never cried before. I felt in that instant, all the years of my brother's underlying pain and anger, even though he had told me this horrible piece of history in the most humble voice. He had shared his feelings as honestly and as straightforwardly as anyone could tell such a thing. In my heart, there was no hesitation to instantly take his side in the matter, the same as I had done my entire life.

He was right about another thing he had said too. Nothing he could say was ever going to change a single thing about the very real experiences we had shared in our lives leading up to this day. I wouldn't change the good, the bad or the ugly—any of it, even with its challenges. And the fact that our lives had ever been given a chance to be good was only as a direct result of the horrible chain of events that Denzil had just told. His decision that night, as a mere child not even yet a teenager, had insured that he, mother and all the subsequent brothers and sisters would have a future.

I tried for a second to picture what kind of life we might have had if he hadn't, in his incredible youthful bravery, made that decision. "I love you Denzil," I blurted out. "I just don't know what else to say, but I love you, Brother. Thank you for saving all of us."

He shook his head. "Well, now. That's about the oddest reaction ever. I didn't expect that."

"I know how things might've turned out if it hadn't been for your decision to follow through on what had to be done. You've always told me, coached me, about following through on things. Jesus, Denzil, even as at ten years old you could do it! Why has it been such a difficult thing for me to learn?"

"People are so different that's all. You're not me and aren't ever going to be. I wouldn't want to know you if you were. What the hell kind of people would we be if we all acted and reacted the same in this life?"

"There's got to be more to this story than this. Do you feel up to telling me more?"

"I don't mean to be mysterious but...no. I can't right now. Getting up to this point is the limit I can manage for today. Come out in the field this Saturday and I'll get my guts up to tell you the rest of what happened that night and in the days that followed. I've got to get back or Bernadette's going to come looking for me out here.

"I know," I said. "I'm so happy for the both of you. Go home to your wife. We'll take this up again on Saturday."

He nodded his head to me quickly and turned to walk away.

I collected my things and followed, purposely keeping a long distance between us so that he could be alone with his thoughts.

At the end of the corn row, he stopped and pointed off into the direction of his truck. "I'm parked over there," he called out to me. "By the way, next Saturday, bring a little nip of gin. I've told you the most intense part of the story, but the rest of it is, as you can imagine, beyond strange."

Suddenly, I wanted to lighten the mood. I ran up to him and grappled my arm around his neck from behind like I always used to do when we were kids. As he struggled to escape me, I rubbed my knuckles around in his hair and knotted it up. Then I said, "Well, from you I wouldn't expect anything else but strange. A nip of gin for us both on Saturday."

I watched him walk towards his truck and thought about what a relief he must have felt to tell me about taking the life of another man, his (and my) own father no less. I wondered why I didn't feel any sense of loss--if it was normal. To think that he had carried this around with him since his childhood was sad. There was something about Denzil that let him carry burdens and big ideas and legitimate worries on his shoulders without ever letting on to anyone if he felt overwhelmed. He was solid and surefooted like no one I had ever met.

CHAPTER NINE

After we had nervously checked to see that the moon was right and the path leading out to the barn was clear, Denzil and I settled ourselves upon the big tractor with a bottle of gin and a couple of short, thick drinking glasses. We sat down across from one another and he launched straight into the remainder of the story that he had come to tell.

"No sense leading into this with any fanfare," he said. "We both know now where I left off before. So to start at the place where I left off is best."

"Yeah, let's just get right into that part," I said. I had mulled the story over enough in my mind by now to realize that I really didn't care about the second part, except to allow my brother to get the burden off of his heart.

"We couldn't bury the body on the farm, for fear it might be visible," Denzil started. "I know it might sound harsh, but Mother feared it would be dug up and there would be consequences for either she or me," he explained.

"That the ensuing investigation would lead to someone separating us. Even some years later if it were found, she told me, an investigation would surely commence. Mother had become, I would say, extremely, extremely unraveled after that night, like a winter sweater that is worn again and again, then one thread becomes loose, then another and another, until there's nothing about it can keep you warm. I suggested we tell Aunt Lucy or Aunt Odette and that they could come over and help us, but she was afraid somebody would call the law. Even though I was still just a child, I realized it was me who needed to stay clear-headed and smart if we were going to avoid trouble over this happening. And I knew that I had it in me to see things through."

"But it was more than just a happening, Denzil," I offered. "This is what the--not me-- would call murder."

"Wasn't murder to put an end to it. Do you honestly think now that it was?"

"No. I didn't mean from your standpoint. I meant from others'. Go on then. You were the one who had to think this through then—what to do?" I poured a bit more of the gin into each of our glasses for us to sip.

I remember that night so clearly, how Denzil told the rest of the story with a strange sort of fearful pride in the craftiness of what he had done. He had resolved to finish what needed to be finished. "I suggested to mother that we needed to quickly build one of those storm shelters that so many other families in Kansas had on their properties—an underground shelter with masonry walls going eight or ten feet under the ground. We'd use the building of that shelter to conceal the body underneath it."

"That's brilliant!" I shouted out.

"Well, it wasn't easy. Was a nervy time after two workmen came first and dug the hole for the foundation, then me having to dig even further after they left. Wasn't easy digging under their work--an additional hole deep enough to conceal a dead body. The ground was rocky. It was lined with that thick dingy grey clay that we know all too well from working out here. I struggled like any twelve-year-old would, gaining inches of progress at a time.

As it happened, that next day the eldest mason became suspicious. Asked me why I was re-digging over their work. He began to question me extensively about what I was up to. I tried to lie, but I guess my face couldn't do it properly. Then this mason let himself into the barn and discovered the body, bundled in sheets and tied tightly, then slipped in plastic, as that is all mother could think of to do.

After mother and I begged and pleaded for this mason not to turn us in, after we had explained every bit of what had happened with the beatings and on the night when everything went wrong. Mother still had plenty of bruises and some cuts too to prove our story. I remember so clearly what he said to us. He said, 'I'm going to help you and we're not, any of us, going to speak about this ever again.' I remember to this day, that this big man who worked with concrete and stones with rough, massive hands like an ogre—that he had tears in his eyes. He really understood what we had been through.

So, from there he and I together finished digging the rest of the hole where I had started. Later, he led mother and I back up to the house so we didn't have to witness him putting the corpse into the ground beneath the storm cellar. Once the walls were being mudded in and the thing started taking shape like a real shelter, I could tell that mother was becoming more at ease, more hopeful each day. I watched her hands which had remained for nearly a week, clasped around her own heart, unfolding.

One evening after the storm cellar project was finally complete--I mean, the walls painted and the metal door installed--I watched her take down her long hair as she sat in the rocking chair. I watched her brush it out and noticed how the color was returning to her face. 'It's a strange land and a strange way for us to begin a new life now, isn't it Denzil?' she had said then, looking so serious at me. 'You're the bravest boy in the world for what you've been a part of here. But listen to me now,' she was saying to me, struggling to not cry when she said it...'Please don't let these events on this farm change your love for our home or change your heart in any way. This is our home and it always will be. Stay the same happy, vibrant and nervy boy you've always been. Do that for me would you? I couldn't stand to think of you any other way. Be strong and let this fade from your memory as I'm going to work hard to put it out of mine.'

I promised her like this; I said, "I will be putting the finish of our abusing father out of my memory. Thing is,

I practically have already done so, from the moment I cracked his evil head. We didn't deserve to be treated like that. I'm glad he's gone forever, if you want to know the truth of it."

She had looked at me straight in my eyes, with both sadness and I could see, a bit of weariness on that evening. No doubt, she knew better than I that no matter what I said, these events would affect me for the rest of my life. Truth is, if it hadn't been for having to deal with it afterward, I don't think I would have left it in my thoughts for even a day. I'd never been so ready to be done with a problem in my very young life or at any time after. That's all he was for mother and me--a problem. Even now, I have no feelings of mercy for men who'd abuse a woman or children. They're low as venomous snakes in a field and deserve to be cut down. Over time, mother relaxed from her edginess. She remarried the father we have come to know and who has been here for us. I do not know what she told him about our first father. She has never spoken to me about it and I do not care. She has been happier too in that sense because our new father, even with his faults, is taking care of us very well. He doesn't hit her and he doesn't steal our money so that we have nothing to eat."

Denzil put his hands on both my shoulders and gripped me hard. "Marc, I don't know why I chose to tell you about this now. I think it must be that these events moved to the forefront of my mind after the war, you know? Like it caused these memories I had put away to rise up in me again."

I released his strong grip on me and wrapped him into a brothers' bear hug. "Telling me was right, Denzil," I said. "Now you're not in this by yourself. I'm going to carry this secret for both of us, too. So...what of the man who helped?" I asked. "Whatever happened to him? How did he live with being part of it?"

Denzil shrugged. "I dunno' how he sorted it out personally, for himself. Only that he lived and died in this town and, as far as I can tell, never spoke of anything. Men in those days kept their word. Sometimes that was all they had to elevate them, separate their character from that of other men. It wasn't like there were different levels of succeeding in the farming business. Being a success back then involved the volume of your crops but also the depth of your character or your word. I'd pass by him in town now and then and we'd connect eyes, give each other a simple nod, adjust our hats or our posture a little and move on."

"Let's do the same then," I said. "We'll move on from this conversation and not speak about it again."

"Thanks, Marc," he said. "I knew if I told you—I'd be free to go forward properly in my life. I didn't want to carry it alone anymore and I didn't want to bring it up again to our mother. She surely had to put it out of her mind in her own way."

"I'll carry this happening, this memory, for you from now on, Denzil," I said. "It is my burden to bear now. I'll bear this for you willingly because I think it's time that you never think about it again. Put it out of your mind completely and get on with the rest of your life. You have so much to look forward to, so much happiness now with Bernadette."

* * *

The winter that year had come roaring in upon a hard, cold wind that blasted across the prairie while we met the challenges head-on in our usual way. Now that it was turning ever-so-slightly into spring, we were emerging from isolation and preparing for the planting season. Everything was going well on the home front, so Bernadette and Denzil had driven their new Chrysler into town to pay a visit to our dear old aunts. The family didn't expect them back until suppertime, so no one thought anything when they were running late, until a neighbor down the road arrived and told us that Denzil had been arrested.

"What for?" my mother asked, placing a hand over her mouth to suppress a gasp.

"Can't be certain," the woman replied. "I just saw the sheriff pulling their car over and watched from a distance. Looked to me like were putting handcuffs on him. That's how I saw that he was being arrested."

Without thinking twice, I jumped into the front seat of the old blue truck and burned up the road leading into town. I'd go to the jail and offer whatever help my brother needed. It never occurred to me to ask about Bernadette. Where was she in all of this? And what in God's name could he have done? Then, a cold wave of fear rushed over me thinking that someone, outside our family, who somehow knew what happened long ago had told the story to the police, after all these years. But Denzil had only been a child back then, so how could they take him in after all? My mind was crazed thinking of his current situation even without knowing how bad it might be.

On the way to the police station, I passed by the Chrysler, stopped on the side of the road just as the neighbor had reported. No one was in it.

I raced on into town, reached the police station and rushed through the double front doors. "Where's my brother," I asked the woman at the front desk. She was a former classmate of mine. I knew I could count on her to help with information.

"None of your brothers are here," she answered, looking puzzled. "Which one anyway?"

"Denzil," I said.

"Why would you think he's here?" she asked calmly.

"Someone said he was arrested this afternoon. I saw his car on the side of the road on the way over here."

"No," she said. "I don't know who told you that, but I would know. He's not here."

"Can I speak to Sherriff Mazur?"

"He's out on a call to a car accident on the other side of the county."

"Look," I said. "If you know something about my brother, you'd better tell me. It's no secret that the Mazur family doesn't care much for us, nor us for them, but I need to know where my brother is."

It was at that moment, that I felt myself transforming from the guy who generally tried to follow the rules to the guy who didn't care what anybody else wanted. I only wanted my brother to be safe.

The desk clerk spoke in a voice that was meant to calm me. "You know I'd tell you, honestly Marc, I sure would. There's nothing going on here."

Without even asking, I borrowed the phone on her desk and dialed up my mother. She didn't have any other information except what the neighbor had told her while I was there. That was it. I had half-decided it was a case of confusion but a panic was spinning around in my brain because it still didn't explain why the car had been left on the side of the road.

I drove like a crazed demon back to where I had seen their car, got out and opened the door to the driver's side. Right away, I noticed that a flurry of papers had been pulled off the seat and had fallen to the ground. Bernadette's purse was still sitting on the seat beside my brother's hat. There were household supplies in the backseat in paper bags from the grocery store. Then I heard a faint cracking sound and a man's voice. Loud arguing came from the thick woods that began about three hundred yards away from the road. I jumped back into my truck and cut a trail down the slope, towards the voices, hanging my head out of the window to locate the sounds. There was no doubt now that one of the men yelling was my brother.

Very quickly, I came upon a scene that I will never forget--my brother tied to a tree naked being whipped with a leather strap by the two Mazur brothers. When they saw me they stood back as if they were waiting for me to get out of my truck. With two of them and one of me I never even considered it. I put my truck in gear and headed straight for them. They ran away together at first then separated into thicker sections of the tree-line where my truck wouldn't fit. I got out of my car and chased them, visually tracking their movements as they ran through the trees, running full speed for at least a half a mile onto an open field, until they outran me.

I returned to my brother and began working to cut loose the rope bindings with the only tool I had which was my pocket knife. It wasn't going quick enough but Denzil seemed incredibly patient, given the circumstances. "Bernadette's up there," he said, pointing when one hand was freed. He had a piece of tape on his mouth that he had obviously managed to loosen while he was tied.

I ripped the tape off completely, then looked up a short hill where there was an old wood supply shed. "What happened?" I yelled out hysterically. "Tell me what's going on?"

"Just go get Bernadette!" he yelled back. "Then come back and get me off this tree."

"I'm sorry, Denzil," I said. "I should have been here with you."

"Go get her like I said, Marc!" he shouted louder. "Just go do it!"

I ran up to the shed, flung open the door and found Bernadette there bound with ropes as well, naked, mouth taped. She had tears streaming down her face. I ripped the tape off and she began to cry uncontrollably. "I'm so sorry," I said, struggling again to cut the thick rope with a mere pocket knife. "Can you walk?" I asked when I had freed her. I took of my long flannel shirt and handed it to her. She put it on and began buttoning it up.

"I can walk," she said, just barely getting the words out.

She followed me down the hill to Denzil who was standing there in all his glory, free of the ropes, examining his lash marks. I was thinking of his dignity and I said, I'll run up to the car and get your jacket for you." Then I spun Bernadette around so she wasn't facing him. Why I was concerned with my brother's dignity at that moment, I don't know.

"She's seen me naked," Denzil said, managing a short laugh. "But thanks. And settle yourself down would you. They're gone." Bernadette rushed to hold on to Denzil.

After a quick back and forth trip for the jacket, I wanted to know what had happened.

"What the hell?" I asked. "Start talking. Tell me the brief version."

"We were coming back from town, when Sherriff Mazur pulled us over. Without even a word, he dragged me out of the car, cuffed me and took me down into these woods where his sons were waiting. Then he drove off and left me here. I had no idea what was going to happen or what Bernadette was thinking up in the car left standing on the roadside by herself. Didn't take long for me to figure it out. It was all a pre-planned attack on me, Marc. We had seen the sheriff out in his police car when we first drove into town and walked inside the grocery store. I knew by the way he looked at me that the bad blood between us wasn't over. Now I know they waited for us to take that same road back home because I saw him sitting on the edge of the road, and when I passed by he put his lights on--called over the horn for me to pull over. I thought he was going to give me a speeding ticket or something. I would've never guessed this." Denzil looked down on his torso and examined the raised welts on his skin.

The front of him carried about ten long raised red marks, near the bleeding point. I turned him around to look at his back. Nothing. He picked his shirt up off the ground and put it on, then his pants. "Hey, at least they didn't take my pants away. Throw them up on the road or something. You know that's why they did this. All those years ago—the skinny dipping incident where we ditched all their clothes when they were swimming with those girls. They still remembered it. Now that's what you call a grudge."

"We're going to burn their damned house down now!" I screamed out. Nice Marc was gone, replaced by a mean raging man with an anger inside me worse than anything I'd ever felt about those guys in our youth.

"We're not going to do anything like that," Denzil said. "I don't know what we're going to do. For right now, I want to get my wife safely home and into a warm bath so that she can relax. Then she and I will talk about this together. Our decision alone will determine what we do. Only you and I and Bernadette will know about this for now, understand?"

"This is crazy. No!" I said. "Mother already heard from a neighbor that you got arrested."

"Well, we're going to simply say it didn't happen. She's older now and she's seen plenty to give her anxiety. We won't add to it over this if we can help it."

"You're going to what? What the hell's happened to you? You're just going to let the Mazurs get away with all of it? Just because their father finally got elected as sheriff?"

"We got away with it, Marc. You, I and Auguste threw their clothes in the river about ten years ago when they were skinny-dipping with their girlfriends. They drove home naked. That's what this is about. They said so when they whipped me with a leather strap, among other things."

"Jesus! I know why they think they had a right to do this. But this and what we did are two extremely far distant things. You don't tie a person naked to a tree and lash them with a strap. That's cruelty and insanity is what it is! You fight one man on one man, if you're going to fight."

"That's in your world, Marc, where everything's fair," Denzil said. "But, I can tell you for certain the world isn't like that anymore. Maybe it never was."

"Well, I can tell you that the former sheriff wasn't like this," I said. "I got to know him fairly well in the years you were away. Our family always had a good relationship with the former sheriff. Hell, we even sold our homemade liquor to him. He wasn't a man who'd participate in some screwed up hateful revenge notion like this."

Bernadette was clinging to Denzil, with her head planted firmly on his shoulders, saying nothing while he continued. "Welcome to this new thing called corruption," he said. "You know the worst of it wasn't the humiliation they wanted me to feel from beating me. The worse was what they kept saying. They were saying, 'Here you go Army hero'. That's the part that is the most disgusting to me—that they would throw out those words as if my time in the war was to be mocked." He shook his head at the thought of it. "Drive us back to our car, now would you? I don't feel like walking up there myself."

"Of course," I said. A thousand thoughts raced through my head all at once. Had it been the stories in the newspaper of my brother's honorable service that contributed to sending them into this rage or was it just a long held grudge? I wanted to drive to the Mazur's family property and settle things myself. Even in my irrational state though, I resigned myself to follow Denzil's direction. The realization of what might have happened if I had not been there to stop it, hit me and I suddenly felt terrified for what could have come next.

I followed in my truck while Denzil and Bernadette drove their car back to the homestead. When they walked inside the house, it was already dark which was a blessing. In the dim lighting with my brother and his wife standing behind me, I helped make excuses for them to Mother and said they had merely had car trouble which the neighbor mistook for an arrest. Her face showed that she didn't believe our story any more than she did when we would get into fights during our teen years. I was sorry that I had been forced to lie to her. They quickly went off to their bedroom upstairs and I too went quietly to mine.

That next day, Denzil told me that he and Bernadette had decided to just let the whole thing go, uncontested. "We'll be even now, the way they see it. I feel it's going to be over now and I won't keep this stupid feud going for the rest of my life," Denzil said. "I'm a grown man and I'm putting to rest this childish shit. I'm going to confront the sheriff though, in his office and tell him it's over now."

"When?" I asked.

"Today. And no; you're not coming. I'm going by myself."

"But you might need me for a witness. What if they do something else to you—even worse?"

"I can manage this," he said.

When my brother confronted the sheriff with his speech intended to end the feud, it backfired. He ended up being arrested and thrown into the local jail. He used his one call to phone the house and Mother answered. "Put Marc on the phone," he said simply. She knew again that something dubious had happened and she handed me the phone.

"What are you being arrested for?" I had to say with Mother standing close by, listening to every word. I didn't care who knew what was going on now. I simply had to get Denzil out of jail.

"He says I came in to the station threatening him. That I was threatening him physically."

"Did you?" I asked.

"No. I told you what I was going to say and that's what I said—that it's over. I'm done fighting. That I thought it was the height of foolishness, not to mention cruel, for grown men to do what they had done to me and to terrify and humiliate Bernadette like that. From that, he escalated me into an argument so that whoever was in the station heard it. I said nothing after that. Next thing I knew he put me in handcuffs again and locked me up."

"This is out of hand. I told you I should've gone with you. Damn it!" I shouted out. I wanted to knock someone down over this. Purposely settling myself inside, I tried to think clearly. "So, there were other people in the station who saw this, who heard what was really happening?"

"Yeah. The woman you knew from school was here and a couple other people sitting at a desk in the front of the station. I was back in his office when this happened, so it was separate from the others. It looked like I went in there to start a fight."

"So what's he charging you with?"

"Threatening a sheriff."

The words fell on my ears and seared into my soul. Denzil, as a former Army captain, had more respect for the law than most people did. I knew it must have been severely disappointing to feel corruption's hand weighing so heavily upon his life. "I'm going to hire an attorney," I said. "Immediately. I'm going to work on this until I get you out of there. Trust me."

"Soon, I hope," Denzil said. "Whatever you do; get the attorney soon." I could hear someone take the phone then and the receiver went dead. I could only hope and pray that no harm would come to my brother while he was jailed.

It wasn't just our parents who were told the entire truth at this point. Someone alerted the newspaper about

Denzil's arrest. The story that followed skipped over his meritorious service in the army and acknowledged that in his youth, he had held a certain reputation locally for trouble. A second story followed, a day later that questioned his mental state. It was worded as if he were the only tenant currently being held in the jail. Then mother, who had finally been told everything from the beginning, visited the jail herself to be sure that Denzil was okay. It was a time of turmoil for all my brothers and sisters who all had to sort out the gossip in town surrounding his predicament. Father stayed back at the farm, never coming into town, never making a single telephone call to anyone about it. It was as if the only contribution to the family he could make was doing what he knew how to do and that was to keep the farming operation running while we were all dealing with Denzil's situation.

In the end, with the help of an astute and angry bulldog attorney, Denzil was released after serving three months in jail. Without even a hearing or a trial, the matter was officially closed. Still, now and then, the local paper would continue to focus on Denzil, writing stories about his wartime heroics one month and pondering what lead up to his time in jail the next. Nobody seemed to know all of the facts and the truth was churned into whatever the minds of our counties residents could conceive.

As soon as one of these locally interesting filler stories would appear, our mother would begin a frantically determined campaign to counter anything written about Denzil with the truth. Eventually, someone else in the town would do something to make them become the more interesting person and Denzil's history would again fade into the background. It was during these campaigns in the defense of her eldest son that I realized where we had all inherited a good quantity of fire in our hearts for fighting. She was relentless in her determination to squash anything untrue or written in a scandalous fashion. After that, the local journalists began to weigh any benefit against what was bound to come from Mother over their writing articles about my brother. For many years, there were no more articles written about Denzil until his obituary.

CHAPTER TEN

I never brought up the subject of our first father's demise with Denzil again, but as a result of what he had told me, I developed a deeper sense of gratitude towards our second father for taking on our family as his own. I wondered if he knew all of the details of what had happened or if he just believed that mother's first husband had simply abandoned us. It occurred to me that the old aunts, Lucy, Odette and Claudette surely knew at least part of the story.

Father being in our lives, first or second, didn't really matter. I saw that now. It was the being there and the taking care of things that I appreciated in him more now. He had taught us so much that was useful for our futures on the homestead and he had done the best he could do. Leaving out any of my usual masked or left-handed references to his drinking or irritable temperament, I found the right timing one day to say to him, out of the blue, that I really appreciated him--that we couldn't imagine life without him. He didn't take the compliment exactly the way I expected but I needed to say it to him all the same, for myself.

Later, when I told Denzil what I had said, just in conversation, he became a bit ruffled like he does when someone isn't thinking as clearly as he expects.

He warned me that Father didn't know the complete story, that Mother had told him her first husband had not wanted a wife and children and had simply walked away one day, never to return.

"I didn't say anything," I defended. "I promised you I wouldn't. I wasn't sure what he knew but I just wanted to let him know I appreciated him being our father."

Denzil wondered how this went. "So what'd he say to that--when you told him how you appreciated him?"

"He just listened--even let me hug him as he sat in his chair, but after that, he went back to his business as if I weren't even there."

"That's like him. Stiff and irritated even when someone's trying to make a real connection with him," Denzil said.

Our father had been 'getting into the whiskey again' as our mother always called it. She couldn't bring herself to say it outright, call it what it was, when he was drunk.

One evening, he had been drinking when he began his usual complaints about all of us children--how we had "grown up without enough discipline" and how "none of us would probably ever amount to much". I used to think that we had grown up stronger because of his rantings, figuring that once we got out into the real world wasn't much anybody would be able to say to tear us down. We had already heard criticism for years inside our own home and his rants had never stopped us from doing anything. But then, on this particular evening, he started in on our mother, tearing her up with his words. That's when I cut in, as I had never done in the past.

"You're mean to her," I said, standing between them. "And it's going to stop. It's going to stop tonight." I looked straight into his eyes and pursed my lips tightly. He saw that I meant business.

"Let it be," Mother said sharply. "He'll settle down in a minute."

"Won't settle down because a woman says so," he said, looking away from me. "In my house, I'll talk as loud and make the rules as I see fit." Then he turned back to me. "A woman like your mother knows it's her job to keep this house up, deal with her children and keep her mouth shut when I say it needs to be."

She flashed a hurt look in his direction. It was similar to the hurt look she had given to my brother and I on those nights so long ago when we had been out drinking-- acting like idiots. I could tell that she preferred if they were going to argue that it would be privately, away from all of us. There was plenty I could have said, but it would have only served to amplify the situation.

My sister Lucy stood up from the dining room though, walked into the living room and stood in front of his chair beside me in a show of unity. She put her hands on the roundest part of her hips defiantly as if she were going to say something.

"Sit your fat ass back down and deal with your own husband, Lucy," our father ordered. "You're married now. You know what it's all about. Of course, just like your mother and your Aunt Lucy, you had to try out a few men along the way before you settled into an honest household."

I should have stood up for my sister, but Lucy was that kind of girl who couldn't be insulted. She would just look at a person who cut her down and laugh as if they were the one outside the norm. This time though, she was angry and although she did retreat, saying nothing, I knew his words had been too much.

I decided I wasn't going to let the comments continue. "An honest household! Well, there's something," I said. "Since you're up for honesty, let's start with you. Why don't you look at yourself? Be honest about the man you are instead of trying to tear us up all the time. When I went to college I studied cases in my psychology classes about the insecurities of men like you. Instead of always finding fault in us, why don't you try to fix yourself?"

He narrowed his eyes and looked at me as if there were an iron question mark hanging over his head. "You're going to change me? Study my head? You want to prod your mother here to change things about me that don't suit her children?" He stood up unsteadily, shaking his finger at me as he spoke. "A woman like your mother here isn't about to change the order of things just because her son went off to college and learned psychology. If you know so much about this psych crap you'd believe then that it's your mother who has the insecurity. She had it when I married her. The response to women's liberation is that the man--the husband--hits the road and never returns. Then women choose the same kind of man that they had the first time. They'll complain, 'Oh he yelled at me' or 'he hit me' or whatever and then go with exactly that kind of man again. They like being treated like less than the man because in reality they are. That's their role in this life."

"Whose reality?" I said, feeling my blood getting hotter by the second. "Yours? Your fucked-up reality?" Because of our mother's strict insistence about it, I had never used the 'F' word in my life, but I felt justified using it now and was in no mood to apologize.

He jumped to his feet faster than I had ever seen him move. He grabbed me by my shirt collar and twisted it up until it nearly cut off my air. "Don't ever throw that word out at me, son," he said. "If you do, I'll make you eat it."

"Don't call me son," I said angrily. I felt his grasp release and I took a few steps backward until I was in my own space again before collecting myself and turning away from him before things escalated further. I moved into the kitchen where Mother, along with Lucy, had retreated. I was glad that even though I was an adult now, I had continued living at the farm. Our family needed me in their corner.

I could hear Mother crying quietly, but hiding the fact by turning her back to me, pretending to towel dry a dish she had just removed from the rack. As she dabbed her eyes, Lucy guarded her from my sight so that whatever dignity she had left could be salvaged.

That confrontation, that one moment I had to say how I felt, changed the way that my father talked to my mother and to the rest of us for a long time. He wasn't so apt after that day, to speak without thinking it through, even if he had been drinking. He knew that there was now a line he couldn't cross with me.

* * *

Eventually, I married a young woman named Elizabeth. Within the first year of our marriage, Elizabeth and I discovered that we weren't going to ever have children. The doctors told us this was 'ninety-nine-percent certain'. It was a great blow to both of us, for we had the same dream that all young couples do. We spoke often about the unfairness of it until we grew resigned to this fact and slowly accepted it.

Shortly after we received our disappointment, the welcome news came about what was to be Denzil and Bernadette's only child. When their baby boy finally arrived about seven months later, he had a full house of aunts, uncles, cousins and farm hands to hold him. Little Michael was born just as busy and full of energy as they say Denzil had been and the physical resemblance was exactly the same. You would have thought that the boy was going to be a future president the way everyone adored and attended to him, including me. I guess it was a natural progression for all of us to roll over our admiration for Denzil onto his child. As Michael began to walk and then run, it was simply delightful to watch him discover each piece of the homestead the same way that each of us had from the time that we learned to walk.

When Michael was five years old one of the cousins handed him a skunk telling him it was a kitty. He was holding it and petting it when mother ran out of the house towards him yelling, "put it down", when the skunk sprayed him from his face to his trousers. He stood there soaked, gasping for breath as mother frantically undressed him, carried him straight into the house and straight up to the bathtub.

As a boy of only five years of age, he now had to endure a confusing ritual—a series of daily baths of tomato juice, lemon juice, various bath salts and other herbal remedies that the old aunts suggested might take the smell away. One of our old German Shepherd dogs had mutilated the skunk right after the spraying happened and for several days, wore the stink of that skunk out in the yard.

Michael's clothes were buried in the ground as an attempt to remove the smell but I don't recall anyone caring to dig them up again to confirm if it actually worked. It was Odette who gladly volunteered to sit with Michael as he laid abed up in his room, reading children's books to him as he isolated until the smell wore off about a week later.

Physically, Denzil's son grew into a near perfect duplicate of his father and every time one of us noted another uncanny similarity between the two, my oldest brother beamed with pride. Wasn't anything that made him more proud than having made the right choice in Bernadette for his wife and watching Michael grow into a fine and honorable young man.

* * *

Mother's heart began to grow weaker with each passing day, then eventually, in the night one evening she passed away from this life to the next. Even as we all saw it coming, it was a terrible blow to us emotionally. It was a struggle to get through the first couple of months without her voice around every corner, without the smell of the things she always baked wafting out of the kitchen. We all took care of our father who also began deteriorating in his health. He grew more frail and weak with each day until he too, passed—just three months later. What we had not realized was that even though he didn't love our mother in the right way—in the way she deserved and the way we all thought he should—he did, in his own way, love her deeply. There was no excuse for his meanness, but he had learned somewhere in his youth that if you didn't control people, they might leave you. After she was gone, his own will to stay on this earth diminished until he simply no longer had reason to live.

The homestead property and the established farming business, which had been in our mother's name for all those years unbeknownst to us, passed by inheritance to all the brothers. Each brother unanimously voted to sign over the property deed to Lucy and her husband with the condition that all the younger siblings could live there as long as they wanted. Lucy would have been happy to have the entire bunch living with her forever, so it was a great decision for all of us. Giving the homestead to Lucy had a higher symbolic meaning to us brothers since she was a woman and since it was a woman, our mother, who had the original vision to accumulate the land. Separately, my brothers and I split the financial assets evenly between ourselves. It was at this time that we began to think about our individual lives and where we were headed.

My sisters, Marne and Odette, eventually married and moved to homes of their own. The twins, Charles and Cain, stayed on at the farm, as did Samuel and his wife. Most of them have passed away, but their extended families continue to live there to this day along with Lucy's children and the families of the six original Mexican braceros who have built their own separate housing on the property. Werner, our German farmhand, ended up marrying a schoolteacher in town. We see him still every Christmastime and consider him as part of our family. My brother Auguste married a Swedish girl, moved to her hometown in Minnesota, and had a boatload of offspring—six kids to be exact. He had never cared much for farming, and seemed to want to move as far away from the memories we made there as he could.

Before I grew too old or too unhealthy to travel, I had to deal with my strong sense of urgency to experience the world outside of our isolated eight-hundred-acre farm too. Number one on my list of places to see was France. I wanted to go there because Denzil had talked about seeing the beauty of the countryside with such astonishment, even in a time of war, and because our dear mother never got the chance to go back to her homeland. I decided to go there for all of us.

"You think there's a life outside this farm that's better?" Denzil had asked me when I told him about my plans.

"I'd like to see if there is," I said. "There's got to be fields of something other than corn to look at."

"Lots of weeds out there in this world too," Denzil said with his typical double meaning.

"No use trying to talk me out of it. I'll go to France and I'll see mother's people's former houses."

"There you go digging up ghosts again. The idea of ancestry has no bearing whatsoever on the life you're living today," Denzil said. "I can promise you that. If you do go to France, go because you want to see the fields of lavender and olive trees. Go to eat fancy pastries of all sorts and drink wine and go fishing with the locals. Now that's a real reason for getting away."

"I'm going to do it," I said. "And I'm gonna' buy tickets today for me and Elizabeth--to make sure I don't change my mind."

"Would you mind taking along another traveler?" he asked anxiously.

"You can't leave Bernadette here at home and go off to Europe with me."

"Not me. I've seen all of Europe I ever want to see during the war. Take Michael, won't you? I'll pay for his ticket. He'd appreciate it and so would I."

Without hesitating I answered, "Of course. He goes with me then."

When Michael and I returned from a month-long tour of France, we were met at the airport by more family members than we had expected. They asked us to sit down in the terminal--said there was some bad news.

I couldn't believe it.

For over twenty years Denzil and Bernadette had loved each other before rounding the corner of a country road one evening and being killed in a head-on car crash by a drunken driver. It seemed such a cruel ending to both of their precious lives and an absolutely painful abrupt end to their son's and my incredible vacation.

In the years that followed, young Michael became my right hand man around my new house in town. In essence, I became his second father, showing him as much love and consideration of his difficult circumstance as I possibly could. I let him know that no matter what he ever needed for the rest of his life, I would always be there. His father, my brother Denzil, had never let me down and I owed his son my devotion without hesitation. I put Michael through four years of college and later stood as best man at his wedding.

* * *

Isn't it funny how you think back about the last words you ever spoke to someone or the last words they ever spoke to you? I have learned that it is important to say the right words at the right time to people because you don't know at the time that they could be part of the last conversation you will be able to have together.

"I'm really proud of you, my brother," Denzil had said to me only a month before he died. "Of all the kids, I thought you'd probably be the one to need the most prop-ups from the rest of us. But you proved you've got balls and brains. Doesn't get any better combination than that."

I had laughed at his view of me at the time. "I've got the balls but you've produced children and I can't–go figure that one," I had said, trying to make light of something that pained me.

He laughed in that wonderful way that was uninhibited and real. "It's the way of the corn again," he said matter-of-factly. "Your lot in life is obviously to be a damned fine uncle to all these nieces and nephews around here, especially Michael."

I think back on those words and I can now accept all things that aren't as I would wish them to be. The world is as it should be, despite our hardships, despite the fact that I still miss my parents and my eldest brother every day. When it was time, I did step up with confidence to be the best uncle I possibly could be. Even though I can't imagine what lies around every corner in this life, I'm still here and there's a reason for it; so I'm going to live every remaining season of my life as it comes.

I doubt that my brother, Denzil, ever adequately measured the significance of his one life. He had, from a very young age, taken on so much weight upon his shoulders. He had instinctively known that by trying and persevering even in the face of hardships, that the rearview mirror would hold an incredible story. I personally, had in my youth, waited to escape our family's homestead in the middle of nowhere for greener pastures, hoping for something extraordinary to happen in my life. He had been content to let whatever came his way define and shape his life without question.

What I had not realized was that my life, as simple as it had been, gave me a depth of experience that I cannot compare to someone else's life. It's when one looks backwards through the years that we realize that truly extraordinary moments were happening the entire time. We didn't all live happily ever after, but collectively, we lived with wild abandon at times and with charity at others. We lived too with passion and with humility. For that I think we all became wealthy beyond measure.

Eventually, I travelled around the world as I had always dreamed of doing. Now, whenever I come back to the old wooden farmhouse, sitting in the clearing at the center of eight hundred acres, it is still the place I consider home. It amazes me that in an era of farmers being forced off their lands or giving up, choosing any life other than the one that demands hedging bets against the cumulative costs of running a farming operation, that the next generation is able to keep it running.

So often farmers now are reliant upon unknown commodity prices or, worse yet choose suicide when everything they've worked for is lost. Our lot somehow kept the landscape changing enough to meet the challenges that came with each passing year. We did it year after year, with a heavy dose of optimism and by pulling together unselfishly. We were not afraid of hard work nor did we dwell on the doubting of things that we couldn't see.

On my most recent visit this year, I wandered out to the cornfield for a moment in the evening, purposely to recall the night that Denzil had finally explained the way of the corn to me. I'm not sure that I fully understood then, what he was getting at, but certainly I do now. On this stretch of Kansas soil, as the earth was bringing forth those towering green ears of beauty wrapped tight in golden silk fibers, we were protected by the grace of God and by each other. Our remoteness also graciously allowed a lot of 'happenings' to be sheltered from the light. That, for us, was just fine.

In the daylight of the next morning, my dear old sister Lucy woke me up to a fantastic breakfast out on the front porch. I noticed that someone had decided to change the paint color of the house from white to a light grey, as if that somehow made it less of a farmhouse and more of a family home.

Since I have moved away, the house itself has had numerous upgrades—for example, there are new bathrooms upstairs and the kitchen has grown an additional thirty feet off the back side. The front porch, screened in now, runs out onto the area where everyone used to park their cars then all the way across the length of the house. The same rocking chairs that mother and I used to sit in and sing songs to each other are lined up neatly there. It gives me great joy to see them. They are solid and grounded like I am, part of it still.

I'm living in Maine now, watching the skiers take to the slopes in the winter and I return to my former bedroom in Kansas for a few weeks every summertime. As I look out the window of the den at my condominium, seated in front of my computer screen, I don't need to wish for inspiration. It comes faster than my old fingers can type. With a smile spread wide over my face and a silent toast with a glass of whiskey to my brother Denzil, I know I have lived my life according to the way of the corn. By digging my roots firmly into the ground every day, I still stand tall and vigilant. I eagerly welcome into my life, both the sunshine and the rain.

Made in the USA
Columbia, SC
09 November 2022

70688649R00143